Samuel Edward Dawson

Letters of "Colonist" on the Government of Public Opinion

SALZWASSER
VERLAG

Samuel Edward Dawson

Letters of "Colonist" on the Government of Public Opinion

Reprint of the original, first published in 1859.

1st Edition 2022 | ISBN: 978-3-37512-216-4

Verlag (Publisher): Salzwasser Verlag GmbH, Zeilweg 44, 60439 Frankfurt, Deutschland
Vertretungsberechtigt (Authorized to represent): E. Roepke, Zeilweg 44, 60439 Frankfurt, Deutschland
Druck (Print): Books on Demand GmbH, In de Tarpen 42, 22848 Norderstedt, Deutschland

rious course is resorted to, the consequences may be disastrous to the peace of this country. There is a limit to all human powers of endurance.

If the inhabitants of this country should again be driven to the *ultima ratio*—the last redress of an insulted people and a constitution trodden under foot by those who are deputed hither to uphold it—the effect may be damaging to British rule on this continent. In the event of such an untoward contingency, there will never again be heard the opprobrious designations of " rebel," or " rebellion," nor a charge of treason against any one. These odious epithets will then have merged into other terms more conclusive and definite in their acceptation and results. History will record the whole affair under another name. Every loyal British subject, however, hopes that the day is far distant when the Canadian people will resort to such an alternative, or that that " gun is to be fired by a French Canadian which is to give the last echo of British dominion in North America," according to the celebrated dictum of that great prophet in his own country, Sir E. P. Taché.—Canada—as a constitutionally governed country —is the first and most important dependency of the British Crown. The Canadians are loyal from principle, loyal from a feeling of self-preservation, and loyal from a just appreciation of the sum of liberty they enjoy under the standard of Queen Victoria, but they will claim the full rights of British subjects as long as it continues to wave over them. Neither English nor French have the remotest desire to barter their freedom for the present degrading thraldom of " Imperial France," or the tyranny of the rabble sovereignties of Columbia. The retention of Canada is the retention of that great seat of empire in the vista which is larger than the whole of Europe, and which is now warmly engaging the public mind on both sides of the Atlantic, and the rights and the attachments of its people are not to be trifled with. While the distinguished nobleman who endeared himself to the Canadian people by his amiability, and his honest, inflexible regard for their rights and liberties, is extending the dominion of England and the sphere of European civilisation in the East :—

LETTERS

OF

"COLONIST"

ON THE

Government of Public Opinion.

~~~~~~~~~~~~~~~~~~~~~~~~~~

THE MACDONALD-CARTIER AND THE CARTIER-MACDONALD ADMINISTRATION : THEIR VICTIM AND THEIR DEFENDERS.

THE MISSION TO ENGLAND.

THE JUDICATURE ACT, AND THE NULLITY OF THE COURT OF QUEEN'S BENCH, L. C.

RUMORS OF A CHANGE OF GOVERNMENT, AND OF A DISSOLUTION.

RUMORS OF A MINISTERIAL POLICY ON THE QUESTION OF THE SEAT OF GOVERNMENT.

THE PENAL PROSECUTIONS AGAINST MINISTERS, &c., &c., &c.

~~~~~~~~~~~~~~~~~~~~~~~~~~

QUEBEC:

PRINTED BY MIDDLETON & DAWSON, FOOT OF MOUNTAIN HILL.

1859.

THE GOVERNMENT OF PUBLIC OPINION.

THE MACDONALD-CARTIER AND CARTIER-MAC-DONALD ADMINISTRATIONS : THEIR VICTIM AND THEIR DEFENDERS.

(*To the Editor of the Quebec Gazette.*)

QUEBEC, 27th September, 1858.

SIR,—T'lat portion of the press of Canada which usually upholds the Government of the day, is now in full blast in defence of the Governor General, upon the stand recently made by him against the Brown-Dorion Administration,— the advisers whom he had himself called to his assistance to enable him to administer the Queen's Government in this Province. Every unworthy epithet and nickname which their polite reading can supply, are unscrupulously and vindictively hurled against the members of that Administration, whilst the most extravagant expressions of laudation are lavished upon the Governor General with a view to shield him from the consequences of the constitutional blunders— not to say crimes—which he has committed against the rights of the people of this country. A storm is gathering around him not only from the press of Canada, but from that of the Lower Provinces, and of England and Scotland, and in the precise ratio of its increase rises the billingsgate in lieu of rational argument on the one hand, and fulsome adulation on the other.

Now, let us analyze the *casus belli* and reduce it to its constituent elements—*a sa plus simple expression.* The question of the choice of a Seat of Government, which appertained to the prerogative of the crown, had been very considerately and wisely left to the decision of the Legislature and Government of this Province. They, after repeated attempts, were unable to arrive at any satisfactory conclusion on the subject, and they referred it back to the Home Government, praying Her Majesty to resume the exercise of her prerogative in this behalf. Instead of selecting that place, or any one of the places, which had received the greatest number of votes of the people's representatives in Parliament, Her Majesty's constitutional advisers, in an evil hour, made choice of an insignificant and newly-fledged city, which happened to be the very *lowest* in the estimation of the Legislative Assembly. Before the promulgation of this decision and the meeting of Parliament, the Administration, which had recommended the reference, had undergone important changes in its composition, and had in truth been entirely broken up, by the retirement from office of eight out of the twelve members of which it consisted at the time of the reference, namely—Taché, (Premier), Drummond, Cauchon, Lemieux, Spence, and Morrison, (members of the Cabinet,) and Ross and Smith, Solicitors General, leaving Macdonald (new Premier), Cayley, Vankoughnet, and Cartier, the sole remaining members of the Government of the reference. Upon the meeting of Parliament the new Government, after having been repeatedly challenged to announce their policy on this important question, declared that they intended to carry out the decision of the Queen. They, with the exception of four of their number, had not advised the reference. They were not, and could not be held responsible as a Government either for the reference or the decision upon it.

The members of the former Government had declared in the House that they should abstain from offering any advice tending in any way to sway the determination of this matter. Yet they permitted the Governor General, the head of the Provincial Executive, and legally and technically constituting in his own person the Government of the Province, to cross the Atlantic and to impose upon the Colonial Minister the selection of Ottawa, in contempt of the opinion of the Assembly, and after that same Minister had declared to several of the delegates sent to England, that that locality was "*quite out of the question.*" Such is the settled belief and conviction of all thinking and unbiassed men in the Province. It was well known that the decision was most unsatisfactory, and that it would be repudiated by an overwhelming majority of the Canadian people. Nevertheless, perfectly conusant of all this, and that a new Parliament was assembled, the members whereof were in no wise committed to the reference by their predecessors, the existing Government—pressed by the same sinister influence through which a selection had been audaciously made upon *ex parte* representations transmitted to England and as yet unknown to the people of Canada, and in despite of the constitutionally expressed opinion of their representatives—the rump of the deceased Government of the reference with their new adjuncts, needlessly threw themselves into the breach to carry out the decision which had been so surreptitiously procured,—an act of folly and blind rashness, which none but a weak and tottering Administration could have been guilty of. Governor and Council combined to sow the wind—*they are now reaping the whirlwind.*

To return :—When the question of the Seat of Government came up in the House, after having been unpardonably suffered to languish during five months, the Ministry adhered to their declared policy, but with amazing magnanimity permitted their friends to vote as upon an open question. After a long and exciting debate, the claim of the vice-regal bantling was duly and formally rejected by a majority of 14. Mr. Brown thereupon moved an adjournment, and challenged the Government to receive the vote as one of confidence or no confidence, and it was so accepted. The move was somewhat out of place and premature ; but it is well known that the honorable mover was entrapped by several of the known partizans of the Ministry (who had voted against them on the Seat of Government,) openly canvassing in the House in favor of the adjournment, and afterwards returning to the rescue and voting against it, thereby giving the Government a majority of *eleven.*

The following morning at ten o'clock, the Ministry announced their resignation as a consequence *of the vote upon Ottawa.*

Their declaration to stand by the act of the Home Government was a blunder, as already shewn; their resignation was blunder number *two*—not to characterise it as something more reprehensible. Mr. Brown was immediately sent for by the Governor General, and the sequel appears in the written correspondence between them, which it becomes necessary in some degree to analyze, in order to extract some light from out the darkness which envelopes it. Usually whe i the Queen's Representative is beached by his Ministry throwing up the reins, it is held to be a distinct avowal on their part that they are no longer in a condition to administer the affairs of the Province. He is then compelled to have recourse to others to advise him in the conduct of the Government, thus suddenly brought to a stand. He summons them to his assistance in extricating himself from the dilemma in which he finds him self. He entreats them to come to *his* rescue, as the burden lies heavily on his shoulders until he shall have accomplished this important task, when his personal responsibility ceases. It is a conjuncture eminently of mutual confidence. The high office which the Governor General occupie. : nd the importance of the services to be rendered to the country by him and the co-laborers chosen by himself, ought naturally to beget mutual respect and reliance, and a strong determination to fraternize, with a view to a cordial co-operation in the great work which they have undertaken, of advancing the prosperity and promoting the welfare of two millions of the Queen's subjects in this Province, constituting, as respects constitutional rights, the most important dependency of the crown. In any controversy or "misapprehension," which may arise in the course of a negotiation of this character, the Governor General has the advantage of his exalted station in shielding him from any suspicion of unfair play, in the absence of any violent presumptions to the contrary. The position is always a delicate and a difficult one, and it was rendered infinitely more complicated in the recent instance by the anomaly of a Ministry resigning immediately after receiving an unmistakeable mark of confidence from the popular Branch. From this singular feature the *bonâ fides* of the resignation has been gravely impugned. We shall see what grounds there are for the imputation either as regards the Ministry, or the alleged complicity between them and their master.

The Governor requests that Mr. Brown's acceptance of office should be " *in writing*, in order that he may be at once " in a position to confer with him as one of his responsible " advisers." *At once*! and before he is sworn! and why " *in writing*" to this particular end ? It was an unusual course, exhibiting a latent distrust at the outset. When, in the common transactions of life, men of great " acuteness," who distrust one another, are desirous of making mutual overtures, they take the precaution of receiving their reciprocal advances " in writing," in order to prevent either party from receding or backing out of his offers. This may be necessary and allowable between men who desire to arrive at a final settlement of conflicting interests, in order that the less " acute" party may not become the dupe of the other. In cases touching the restitution of stolen property, for instance, the negotiations are usually conducted in the most guarded manner, lest any one of the " high contracting parties" should be entrapped by the other. But in a matter concerning the formation of a Government, when the Queen's representative selects men of known respectability and integrity to share with him the cares of state, and by whose advice he impliedly declares he shall be governed, the same amount of precaution would not seem to be required ! !

The Governor addresses himself to Mr. Brown as "the most prominent member of the Opposition." Why this designation of Mr. Brown, *in limine*, in a note to himself as a justification for sending for him ? If he was the person most likely to command a majority in the House, the act of the Governor needed no such apparently limited designation. *Cela va sans dire.* If he could not carry the House with him, as the Governor himself afterwards states, the simple act of sending for him, necessarily and obviously, in the opinion of every impartial man, was equivalent to a clear and distinct understanding, on his part, to place the prerogative at the disposal of Mr. Brown and his Cabinet, in furtherance of any

8

constitutional remedy to be suggested by them to enable them to perform the duties which the Governor had solicited them to undertake.

Mr. Brown was sent for on Thursday, the 29th July. On Saturday, the 31st, he formally accepted the task of forming a ministry. It was well known in Toronto on Sunday afternoon (1st August,) that a cabinet had been formed, contrary, as it was currently reported, to the expectations of the Governor and his friends. On that evening, at ten o'clock, the Governor transmitted a note to Mr. Brown. In his note to Mr. B. of the 29th July, he had intimated that " his first object would be to consult Mr. B. as to the names of his future colleagues, and the assignment of the offices about to be vacated, to the men most capable of filling them !" (Let that pass—it is too flat to be commented upon.) In his note of Sunday evening, he requests Mr. B. to " communicate the (enclosed) memorandum to his future colleagues" (without having received any information as to the names or capabilities of those important personages,) " in order," he says, " to avoid all misapprehensions thereafter." Strange that there should run through the whole affair, on the part of His Excellency, such a dread or anticipation of " *misapprehensions* " ! ! In this memorandum he distinctly intimates his determination *not* to dissolve. When asked, he will give his reasons. He has no objections to a prorogation *on certain conditions.* In short, he begins to dictate. He has no objection to abide by their advice, provided they will first follow *his.* He points out the measures of his late Government which must be matured (before he will allow a prorogation,) " subject, of course, to such modificaitons *as the wisdom of either House may suggest* " ! Very condescending this ! " A prorogation is the act of His Excellency." So it is—and so would also be a dissolution or any other act of his ; but to be constitutional, it must be previously determined upon by his sworn advisers, otherwise he, *suo periculo*, assumes the entire responsibility. On the next day, (Monday, 2nd August,) Mr. B. informs the Governor General for the first time that he has formed an administration, and is prepared to submit the names, but declines discussing any measures, or any questions of public policy, until they shall have been sworn and constitutionally responsible for their advice. On Monday at noon they are inducted into office. On the evening of the same day adverse votes are given against the new Administration in both Houses, and on the following day the Brown-Dorion Cabinet, as a matter of course, recommended a dissolution.

Next follows the memorandum of the Governor General of the same day. This is a document *sui generis*: " His " Excellency is bound to deal fairly with all political parties ; " but he has also a duty to be performed to the Queen and " the people of Canada paramount to that which he owes to " any one party, or to all parties whatsoever." " The question for His Excellency to decide is—not what is advantageous or fair for a particular party, but what, upon the whole, is the most advantageous and fair for the people of the Province !! " With the enunciation of a doctrine of this character, it is useless to follow him through this long, argumentative, rambling paper.

The Governor General -- commissioned hither by his Sovereign to administer her government according to the principles and the practice of the British constitution as it obtains in the government of his Royal Mistress, and according to the well-understood wishes of the people of this Province as expressed by their delegates in parliament—constitutes himself the exponent and the arbiter of what is " most advantageous and fair" for that people, and—aping the arbitrary mandates without the sagacity of a Napoleon—reads an incoherent homily to his constitutional advisers, and arrogates to himself the power of dictating to them the course which they are to pursue, and the measures they are to propound to parliament. It is manifest that he is unacquainted with the rudiments of constitutional government. The servile press will term this personal abuse ; and having no other ground upon which to make a stand in his favor, they laud him to the skies as an independent Englishman, a gentleman, and a scholar. Granted that he possesses these high attainments ; but what have they to do with the question at issue ?—Whether he be

English, Dutch, or Arcadian, gentleman or boor, scholar or pedagogue, is perfectly immaterial to the people of Canada; provided he possess sufficient knowledge of the attributes of an independent English statesman to teach him to respect the rights of British subjects,—sufficient *savoir vivre* to restrain him from gratuitously drawing invidious distinctions between the inhabitants of the two sections of the Province, or wounding them in their national traditions; and sufficient constitutional learning and logic to enable him to hold the helm of the vessel of state without intermeddling with the province of the Sailing Master and his crew. One word, *en passant*, upon the scholarship as evidenced in these bulletins. There are to be found in them slight errors of style and grammar, which are certainly highly excusable in a matter concocted with more celerity than deliberation, and which, in fairness, ought not to be noticed. But it is imprudent in the scribes to challenge criticism by invoking the superior *scholarship* of the author.—In the circumstance of the present crisis his penetration was at fault in not seeing that the resignation of his ministry in the face of a decided vote of confidence in their favor, was either an insult to their own supporters, or was fraught with some latent sinister design to recover their forfeited offices, thereby placing him in a false and embarrassing position. In all probability the *compte rendu* to his principals of his clumsy passage-at-arms with the Brown-Dorion administration, is accompanied with a tender of his resignation; if not, common prudence would dictate this course, as the storm of condemnation from which his ministers, past and present, are now fleeing like Mother Carey's chickens across the Atlantic, may necessitate an alternative which might render him ineligible to represent his Sovereign in any other of her dependencies.

The parasites of the topsy-turvy cabinet are blattering extensively on the supposed insult or discourtesy to the Queen in repudiating the selection of Ottawa as the Seat of Government. This act of Her Majesty is but the act of her constitutional advisers. As such it is subject to comment, animadversion, or censure by the people, quite as much as would be any other untoward exercise of the prerogative; and its counsellors are made amenable to the bar of public opinion to answer for their advice, on the fundamental maxim that the "Queen can do no wrong." Whenever wrong is done, or gross error committed, those who are sworn to counsel her honestly and wisely are made to pay the penalty of their transgression.

The thunderer of Printing House Square, who arrogates to himself the office of supreme dictator in matters of state, has allowed himself to be drawn into the egregious blunder of casting obloquy on the people of Canada for the course taken by the Assembly on this question. When Her Majesty exercises her prerogative in respect of any appointment, such as that of the Chief Justice of the Queen's Bench, the Commander of the Forces, or any other high and important public functionary, to whom would the blame of an injudicious selection attach? To the *Queen*—say the lackeys and the thunderer, to serve their own purpose for the nonce. Should Her Majesty in such a case—instead of choosing one of the fittest men in the profession to discharge the duties of one of the highest legal functionaries in the kingdom, capriciously confer the appointment upon some unworthy favorite without character, ability, or legal standing, would not the people of England be permitted to remonstrate against such an abuse of the prerogative? In the present instance the Queen was imposed upon, and they select a city repudiated by the Legislative Assembly, and, as a natural consequence, that Body, as the guardians of the rights and liberties of the Canadian people, declines to abide by the choice. If this course be deemed *discourteous* to the Queen, it would have been equally discourteous to have disapproved of the selection of Penetanguishene, at the western extremity of the Province, or a site on the outlandish and barren coast of Labrador, its *ultima thule* on the north-east, for the same object, had such been the decision ; for the choice was of course unlimited, and the constitutional right to disapprove would undoubtedly have been precisely the same. The people of this Province exercise no control over Her Majesty's imperial cabinet, but they held the colonial Administration answerable for the sin, and drove them to resign, until—like the tiny antomata on a hand-organ, they faced about and slunk back to their former positions. "Insult and discourtesy" indeed! where the people's inalienable rights are trampled upon, and the judgment of the Queen's ministers swayed by backstair influence ! The " insult and discourtesy," if any there be, consist in affixing upon our Gracious Sovereign the odium of a decision which is solely attributable to the stolidity of her colonial minister and the presumption and audacity of her colonial shadow.

Canada, of all the dependencies of the Crown of England, led the van in wresting from the Imperial Government the full concession of that constitutional form and practice of government which has raised England to her present exalted position among the kingdoms of the world. Should the principles evolved in the Brown-Dorion controversy be supinely and tamely acquiesced in, the question arises, whether we have advanced or retrograded in our appreciation of that inestimable boon. If the inhabitants of Canada are true to their instincts, they will denounce this invasion of their dearest rights, and adopt such determined and energetic measures as will speedily " nail the rap to the counter," and for ever prevent a recurrence of the outrage. Public opinion is fast running in the right direction. The statesmen of England are too clear-sighted to permit the rights and privileges of colonists to be jeopardized by any empiric who happens to be decked in the uniform of Downing Street. When the tide of public opinion, backed by sound reason and impelled by a sense of wrong, sets forcibly in one direction, it is a perilous undertaking to impede or dam its onward course. The obstruction but augments its volume and its impulse, until, overleaping all bounds, its accelerated course sweeps every obstacle before it. There is wisdom in foreseeing the descending torrent, lest it overflow its natural bounds and unnecessarily and recklessly cause irremediable mischief. The democratic tendency is ever onward, and perhaps downward in the scale of society, and the impetus given to it by the follies of the minions of power may sap the pillars of our revered constitution, ere we know upon what ground we are standing. Should such unhappily be the *denouement*, the arrogance and the insipid whimperings of the Morning Chronicle, Pilot, and other servile prints, as well as the remonstrances and anathemas of just men, will be alike unavailing to stay the storm.

THE MISSION TO ENGLAND.

(*To the Editor of the Quebec Gazette.*)

QUEBEC, 11th October, 1858.

SIR,—In my last I proffered a few observations on the recent crisis, tending to bring under review the unconstitutionality of the course adopted by the Governor General towards the Brown-Dorion Administration, nicknamed by the subservient supporters of the topsy-turvy cabinet—"the Government of forty-eight hours"! *Il rit bien qui rit le dernier.* It appears now that the newly installed Premier has been deputed by his colleagues to England as a delegate to represent the interests of Canada in regard to the contemplated inter-colonial railway, and the union, federal or legislative, of the British North American Provinces. It has become rather fashionable within late years for the members of the Colonial Government to abandon the high posts assigned to them by the people, and to seek recreation in scampering across the Atlantic, under the pretext of conferring with the Home authorities on matters connected with the welfare of Canada. This, in certain important emergencies, may be highly necessary and advantageous; but we have an undoubted right to be satisfied that the individuals selected for such missions should be public men of ability and standing, and who possess the confidence of the people. The Hon. George Etienne Cartier is the statesman who has lately taken his departure for England as the delegate of this Province. I do not mean to detract from the personal reputation of this gentleman as a member of society, considered apart from his political position and character. But when the interests of this great Province are entrusted to any man, whether a member of the reigning Administration or not, the selection ought to be of a person possessing the highest qualifications for the task confided to him, and whose antecedents are calculated to impress the Government to which he is accredited with the conviction that he is one whose nomination is acceptable to the people in whose name he acts.

Now sir, a short retrospect of Mr Cartier's political career will be amply sufficient to show that he is by no means the individual whom we should have fixed upon as our representative on this occasion. In the previous parliament he represented the county of Verchères in the neighbourhood of Montreal. He at that time filled the office of Secretary of the Province, and subsequently that of Attorney General for Lower Canada. I enter not into his fitness or unfitness for these offices, as it would be foreign to my present purpose. Mr. Cartier was a practising barrister resident in the city of Montreal. At the last general election he aspired to the representation of that city as the first commercial city of Canada ; but of the six candidates who entered the arena, Mr. Cartier, with all the influence of his new position as twin-premier, was found to be the *lowest* in the estimation of the electors, who withheld their suffrages from him, preferring to bestow their confidence upon men of comparatively inferior note. Having been thus signally—indeed ignominiously for a Prime Minister—rejected by the electors of Montreal, he was constrained to fall back upon the rural and more humble constituency of Verchères, which had previously returned him as their representative. After a sharp contest, in which, it was said, every species of corruption was resorted to in his favor, he got elected by a majority of *thirty* ! It will be remembered that at this time he occupied the office of Attorney General for Lower Canada, and the post of twin-premier for Canada in the Macdonald-Cartier administration, formed upon the retirement of Col. Taché (late Premier,) who complacently played into the hands of Mr. Cartier with a view to favor his promotion in the Government. His opponent at Verchères was a Mr. Préfontaine, a respectable *habitant* or farmer, but a man of little education and of no experience beyond the sphere of his humble homestead. Within the time prescribed by the recent statute, Mr. Préfontaine succeeded in serving a notice of contestation upon his Government opponent, after previous repeated attempts to this effect, in which, it is said, he was foiled by the dodging of the Minister to escape a trial. On the meeting of Parliament Mr. Préfontaine prosecuted his contestation, being apparently determined to make war upon Mr. Cartier's thirty votes, but was met by an objection taken by the latter to the recognizance, namely, that the jurisdiction of the officiating magistrate did not appear in the acknowledgment of the suretyship. The recognizance was declared insufficient, and Mr. Cartier retained his *thirty* votes and his seat in the House.

When responsible Government was conceded to Canada its reign was inaugurated under the auspices of LaFontaine and Baldwin, men of acknowledged ability, integrity, and patriotism, who would have scorned to retain their high position under such a sentence of ostracism as that so emphatically pronounced against the present premier. Every act of theirs, private and public, is a guarantee that they would have preferred an honorable retirement into private life, rather than owe their elevation to a merely nominal and fictitious majority of thirty *Esaus* who had bartered the interests of their country for a mess of pottage. The LaFontaine-Baldwin Government and every member of it, would have disdained to avail themselves of a paltry legal quibble to evade a scrutiny of *thirty* votes, and would have forthwith challenged the humble Cincinnatus of Verchères to meet them at Philippi, there to abide the issue of a fair and honorable contest. Not so the man who now presents himself on the vestibule of the Colonial office as the incarnation of the suffrages of the Canadian people— the premier of the Government of two millions of British subjects—a legal luminary with a tail of *thirty* votes, corruptly obtained over an humble tiller of the soil, who was filched of his right of contestation by a miserable objection utterly unworthy of the position of the man who had the meanness to resort to it.

The next phase in the political career of this statesman is recorded in the disgraceful shuffle for office lately perpetrated under the sanction of Her Majesty's Representative, (who "deals fairly with all parties") by the wreck of a former Administration, which had been thoroughly routed and broken down at a recent general election upon a dissolution provoked by themselves, and who are now writhing under the lash of an indignant press and an outraged people.

The Governor General was well acquainted with the political antecedents of his Premier. He well knew that the "shuffle" which placed him at the head of the galvanized rehash of the Macdonald-Cartier Administration, was principally due to his inordinate aspirations, his overweening vanity, his narrow-minded policy, and his virgin innocence of all constitutional and statute law. This, however, is the statesman whom our "fair-dealing" Governor has despatched to the Imperial Government, charged with a mission which, however feasible and laudable in itself, His Excellency was blind enough not to see is designed as another "super-subtle" stratagem to out-manœuvre the member for Toronto, whose star, to their utter discomfiture, is now manifestly in the ascendant.

In any case it will be deemed an arrant piece of presumption in the present Government—master and crew—to have taken the initiative in a matter fraught with such important results to the people of Canada. If the assent of the Legislature and Government of this Province is to be given to a scheme for their federal or legislative union with the other British North American Provinces, it must be effected under the auspices of men possessing the confidence of the people, and not by the trickery of the charlatans of the hour, who shrunk from an appeal to their constituents, and are now banded together to cling to power, *par fas aut nefas*, and to the enjoyment of their forfeited offices. Their foolhardiness is the more reprehensible and offensive to the people of Canada in consequence of the re-election, by overwhelming majorities, of all the members of the Brown-Dorion Administration, in despite of the most strenuous efforts made in every county to defeat them by the Cartier-Macdonald party. It is impossible now to ignore the fact that public opinion, in every county, town and hamlet in Canada, has "decerned" against the "shufflers" in unqualified terms. They possess neither sufficient influence nor daring to make any change in their beleaguered wigwam, lest the necessary resort to any one constituency of Canada should add another defeat to their previous disasters. When Napoleon placed the diadem of the Cæsars on the head of his infant son, he pronounced the significant warning : "*Gare qui la touche !*" Comparing great things with small, we have an illustration of a similar warning in this remote corner of the world in the inverse ratio of potentate and people. Dame rumour has tendered to an M.P.P. of the district of Quebec, the portfolio of the Provincial Secretary, in the room of a member of the Cabinet about to be otherwise disposed of, and it is said that after consultation with his constituents, he still hesitates to accept, or has positively declined the honor. The same authentic source points to another Representative from the same district as an aspirant for the same arduous charge, and a *pis aller* in this government dilemma ; and he also is said to have felt the pulse of the people with the same blighting effect. But whether these reports be well or ill-founded, one thing is most certain, and altogether beyond the domain of Dame rumor, that as to this hapless portfolio, which has gone a-begging for two months, the universal voice of the district of Quebec among parties of every kind and hue, is, in the emphatic menace of the great Napoleon—"*Gare qui la touche !*"

THE JUDICATURE ACT,

AND THE NULLITY OF THE COURT OF QUEEN'S BENCH, L.C.

(To the Editor of the Quebec Gazette.)

QUEBEC, 22nd October, 1858.

Sir,—The system of Judicature lately inaugurated by the present Administration is being fully discussed among the profession and the public in a manner not to crown the " shufflers" with fresh laurels. Within a short time past we have heard it stated that some doubts have been raised touching the legal existence of the Court of Queen's Bench. Rumours of doubts upon a point of such grave importance must not, however, be permitted to continue. If they be really without foundation, they ought at once to be checked and eradicated. If they present themselves in such a shape to men of legal knowledge as to require deliberation, the attention of the constituted authorities ought to be drawn to the question without delay. Should they be found to shake the legality of that high and important Tribunal, a remedy— speedy and effectual—must be instantly resorted to, as the consequences which obviously flow from such a judicial dilemma are truly of a serious and appalling character. Let us at once, then, present to the public a brief synopsis of the Statutes creating that Court, in order to furnish the means of arriving at some correct conclusion in the matter.

STATUTES.

12 *Vic., Cap.* 37.—(1849.)

(A.)

SEC. 2.—By the second section of this Statute it is enacted " That there shall be, and there is hereby established, in and for Lower Canada, a Court of Record, to be called ' the

Court of Queen's Bench,' and *to consist of four Judges* ; that is to say, of a Chief Justice and three Puisné Judges, to be appointed from time to time," &c.

(B.)

Sec. 10.—Three Judges to form a quorum.

(C.)

Sec. 17.—Court to make a Tariff and Rules of Practice.

(D.)

Sec. 24.—Former Courts of Queen's Bench abolished, and " Court of Queen's Bench *hereby established*, and the Judges thereof to have original criminal jurisdiction throughout Lower Canada, and in the several Districts thereof, in like manner" as former Courts of Queen's Bench.

20 *Vic., Cap.* 44.—(1857.)

(E.)

Sec. 6.—By the sixth section of this Act (in force by Proclamation from 24th November, 1857,) it is enacted that " so much of the second section of the Judicature Act of 1849, chapter 37, (vide *supra* A.,) *as limits the number* of Puisné Judges of the Court of Queen's Bench for Lower Canada to *three*, is hereby *repealed*, with the fourth section of the same Act ; and in addition to the Chief Justice and *three* Puisné Judges mentioned in the said section, there *shall* be a *fourth* Puisné Judge of the said Court, to be appointed and qualified in like manner as the other Puisné Judges, and with like powers, duties and salaries."

(F.)

Sec. 8.—Tenth section Act of 1848 repealed, and quorum to be *four* instead of *three*.

(G.)

Sec. 15.—*Four* terms in appeal, and error established at Quebec ; and *four* at Montreal in each year, instead of *two*.

(H.)

Sec. 18.—(Second clause) :—When cause heard by *four* Judges only, and three not concurring in judgment, cause may be reheard, and when reheard, and the other Judge fifth) disqualified, Superior Court Judge may act.

(I.)

(Third clause quoted by reason of the terms used) :—" And the said section" (No. 3, Act of 1851 cap. 88) "So amended" (viz : by clause 2 of this section 18—vide *supra* H ;) " Shall be read as part of the said Act of 1851, which shall apply to the Court of Queen's Bench, *as hereby constituted*, and to the *five* Judges thereof."

(J.)

Sec. 21.—" The said Court in appeal and error, shall be a Court of error in criminal as well as in civil cases, and shall have jurisdiction in error in all criminal cases before the said . Court, on the Crown side thereof," &c.

(K.)

Clauses 21 & 22, 26 to 28, 30 to 32, 60 to 62, and several others, make important changes in the jurisdiction and powers of the Queen's Bench, as constituted by the 20 Vic.

(L.)

Sec. 149.—" The provisions of this act, and those of the several acts therein referred to upon similar subjects, shall be construed with reference to each other, and as parts of the same law, and the 113th section of the judicature act of 1849, chapter 37 (vide *infra* M.) and all other provisions for the interpretation of that act shall extend to the interpretation of this act ; and the express repeal of particular provisions of former acts shall not be construed as continuing in force any other act inconsistent with this act, but any such provision shall be held to be repealed."

(M.)

(113 Sec., 12 Vic., cap. 37.)—" The interpretation act will apply to this act, and all the provisions thereof shall be liberally construed, so as best to promote the attainment of justice in every case, and no construction shall be deemed right which shall leave any provision thereof without effect," &c.

(N.)

Sec. 152.—5th Clause.—" And in like manner the coming into force of the whole or any part of this act, shall operate no change in the *local jurisdiction* of the Court of Queen's

Bench in and for any of the present districts, in the exercise of its original criminal jurisdiction, &c." : until the day which shall be named as that on which this act shall take full effect in criminal matters, in the first proclamation to be issued as mentioned in the fourth section of this act."

Such are the portions of the Statutes relating to the Court of Queen's Bench, which seem to bear upon its constitution.

It is said by those who impugn its legal existence, that in as much as the clause (sec. 2) of the statute of 1849, which enacted that this court should consist of *four* Judges, that is, of a Chief Justice and *three* Puisné Judges, is absolutely repealed by sec. 6 of the act of 1857, (supra E,) and that the same repealing clause enacts that there should be a *fourth* Puisné Judge appointed, the two statutes (being made parts of the same law, s. 149), are to be now read and interpreted as enacting in positive and distinct terms that the Court shall consist of *five* Judges, that is, of a Chief Justice and *four* Puisné Judges, and that therefore the Court cannot be legally constituted until the *fifth* Judge be appointed; precisely as if under the Act of 1849, *three* Judges only, instead of *four*, had been appointed, the Court of Queen's Bench created by that Act could have acquired no legal existence as a Court until the number of Judges directed by the Act had been duly appointed. Further, that this view of the Statute derives confirmation from the terms used in the 3rd clause of the 18th section (supra I,) which refers to the Court of Queen's Bench *as thereby established* and the *five* Judges thereof. Also, that the several sections of the same Act alluded to in paragraph K above, and which confer additional powers on the Court, are indications of the same intention, in as much as, on the supposition that these powers (some of which have in truth been already acted upon,) should remain in abeyance until the appointment of the fifth Judge, such a mass of confusion would be created as to place such a supposition entirely beyond the intention of the Legislature. It is further alleged that the clause 113 of the Act of 1849 (M. supra), which enacts that " all the provisions thereof should be liberally construed, so as best to promote the attainment of justice in

every case, and that no *construction* thereof should be deemed
right which should leave any provision thereof without effect,"
and all the other interpretation clauses, which are loosely and
raggedly drawn in and re-imbodied as so many safety-valves
in the Act of 1857, afford no relief in the present dilemma,
in as much as the legality of the existence of the Court itself
is no question of " *construction*" of any one of the remedial
provisions of the Act ; and that the " provisions" mentioned
in the said section 113 of the Act of 1849, have reference to
the various enactments and " provisions" of the law as a
remedial statute, when interpreted and about to be adjudica-
ted upon by a Court duly and legally constituted, and have
no bearing upon the question of the composition or constitution of the Court itself.

On the other hand, it must not be forgotten that we have a
very formidable answer to all these objections in the fact, that
the four honorable Judges appointed under the Act of 1849
have continued to exercise jurisdiction without the addition of
the fifth Judge ; and when it is considered that they have
deservedly attained to eminence in the profession of the law,
we have a strong presumption that they consider themselves to
be in the full and undeniable possession of the powers and
jurisdiction which they have continued to exercise. Nevertheless—amid the confusion caused by the incessant " tinker-
ing" of the judicature system of Lower Canada for several
years past—it is perfectly possible, that in the absence of their
attention having been in any way called to such an objection,
which naturally no one would anticipate or even dream of, a
radical and serious defect in the constitution of the Court
might remain unnoticed, without attaching blame to any one
of those who administer its functions. We have had various
innovations introduced, and proposed to be introduced into
the system by men of high legal attainments and standing,
which have considerably tended to enhance the proverbial un-
certainty of the law. We have had the code Viger, the code
Stuart, the code Lafontaine, the code Smith, the code Drummond, and last and assuredly least in excellence, the code
Cartier ;—and so in all probability the thing will wag until

we find a Ministry possessed of sufficient discernment to imi
tate the example of other countries in their mode of reforming
their systems of judicature; and an Attorney General endow-
ed with just as little egotism as will induce him to forego the
empty and more than doubtful honor of transmitting his
name to posterity on the back of a mere *brochure* in the form
of a code of judicature, which never does, and in the nature
of things never can survive his consulship. Let them have the
wisdom and the patriotism once for all to appoint a Commission to examine into and consolidate the whole system, and
put an end to these perpetual changes which only invest the
innovator with an access of patronage dangerous to himself
and colleagues, and which invariably tend to create a desire
in the *new* man to overthrow the labor of his predecessor. No
such feeling would exist in regard to a Commission composed
of the ablest men in the profession. Their work would not
be exposed to such damaging vicissitudes.

As the matter now stands, the more we seem to progress,
the more in reality we retrograde. The old Judicature Act
of 1794, and all the statutes of that day, were ably and elabo-
rately drawn. Their vitality was not left to the caprice of
any political empiric who chooses to pull the strings at his
own convenient season in the shape of a Proclamation, for
which we may rummage all the dusty corners of a lawyer's
office without finding it, and which is not even to be seen in
the Statute Book of the succeeding year;—thus leaving us
without any reliable and ready means of ascertaining the
birth-day of the bantling to which it imparts existence. There
is scarcely a practitioner to be met with who will not declare
that the old system, coupled with the excellent rules of practice of the late Chief Justice Sewell, were infinitely superior
to all the voluminous and verbose enactments which have
since overloaded the Statute Book. One thing is most certain, that the present Judicature Act, with its endless amendments of amendments, is daily and universally anathematized
as the most incongruous and impracticable system with which
any civilized country could be inflicted.

Now, sir, no one will rejoice more than the writer, if it can
be shewn that the objections raised to the legal existence of

the Court of Queen's Bench are groundless—a consummation to be desired by every man who is capable of sinking all minor considerations in the welfare of his country and the honor of its Judiciary. For the mere mention of a doubt as to the legality of the acts of our highest criminal tribunal, under whose fiat some of our fellow men have been made to terminate their existence upon a scaffold, and despatched to a bourne beyond the reach of any declaratory Act, is of itself calculated to do infinite mischief, and imperatively demands that the veriest rumor of such a fatality should be instantly and effectually brushed away. Were the Court originally duly constituted, the acts of a Red Indian openly and publicly sitting as a member of it without commission or authority, might be held to be good; but can the principle of the judge *de facto* be made applicable to the case of a whole court not originally legally constituted? It is said *judicis est ampliare jurisdictionem*; but although *all* jurisdiction is said to have been originally a usurpation, no maxim has been handed down to us to shew that he can improvise a jurisdiction, or invest himself with the function of exercising it without express authority.

It is to be hoped that some members of the profession, whose learning and experience qualify them for the task, will devote a small portion of their time to the study and elucidation of this question. Should there be a failure to shew to the satisfaction of men versed in these matters, that the strictures thus offered to the public are without the shadow of a foundation, and that there really exist some grounds for disquietude in the public mind, the first and obvious course is for the Governor General, who represents the fountain of justice in this Province to require a full report on the subject for the use of the public, at the hands of his law officers—the Attorney General for Upper Canada, and the Solicitor General for Lower Canada —the only legal advisers within his reach at the moment; for the other two are now—one, the author of the evil, if such it be found to be, dancing attendance at the Colonial Office, on a mission foreign to the duties of his office, and the other— not yet *in esse*. This is not a point on which there need be any shuffling as between Upper and Lower Canada. It is simply a question of the interpretation of a statute, which the Attorney General for Upper Canada ought to be, and we believe, is as capable of solving as any jurist of Lower Canada. Such a course will not impose any embarrassing task upon Sir Edmund Head who, it is said, claims to be somewhat versed in the *apices juris* as an English Barrister, and is in all probability quite competent to investigate and determine the question himself. It is really too serious a subject to be made the sport of political antagonism, or to be charged upon his Excellency in addition to the long catalogue of responsibilities which now gravitate so heavily upon his vicarious shoulders. His newly-fledged premier is alone answerable for the delinquency.

Should the views above enunciated on the present constitution of the Court of Queen's Bench be found to be just, it is manifest that important consequences must flow from them in a political point of view, which may form the subject of future comment.

PUBLIC DINNERS AND DEJEUNERS.

IS THE HEALTH OF THE GOVERNOR GENERAL A POLITICAL TOAST?

(To the Editor of the Quebec Gazette.)

QUEBEC, 1st November, 1858.

SIR,—In all the dependencies of the Crown it has been almost the invariable custom at public dinners and *réunions* of that nature to toast the health of the person administering the Government, as being the representative of the Sovereign, without reference to distinction of party ; and this very commendable practice has prevailed even in the colonies enjoying free institutions, notwithstanding the necessary existence therein of two or more political antagonistic parties, some of them more or less at war with the colonial authorities. This custom has obtained on the very laudable ground that at the social board all allusions to politics are very properly and by necessity deemed not orthodox, and the toast has thus always been considered as non-committal, and as a mere expression of loyalty to the Sovereign, conveyed through the person of her *locum tenens.* The Queen of England, " upon whose dominions the sun never sets," has always exhibited an example of queenly propriety and constitutional forbearance, in respect of all party movements, which some of her petty Lieutenants would do well to imitate. Charles the First lost his head in consequence of his arbitrary rule and his lending himself to the machinations of party and of the " strategists" of the day. The lesson has not been lost upon his successors. The respect usually paid to the Queen's vice-gerent on all public occasions is essentially based upon the co-relative obligation of

non-interference in local dissensions. But if the head of the
Government, forgetting his high position and his oath of office,
descend into the arena of party strife, and make common cause
with either of the belligerents against the other, he forfeits his
title to respect as an impartial Representative of royalty, and
the rule usually observed in this behalf is necessarily abroga-
ted. When a person of distinction comes amongst us, like the
immortal defender of Kars, whose valor and noble conduct as
a British General his very enemies delighted to honor, and
that the inhabitants of any city are desirous of giving him a
hearty welcome, as a token of the high admiration in which he
is deservedly held, everything ought to be done which is calculated to unite all parties in the common object, so as to
make the demonstration as general as possible, and therefore
the more acceptable to the object of it. In such *impromptu
réunions*, which partake rather of a private and personal than
of a public character, a long and labored list of toasts is quite
uncalled for, and they ought to be restricted to that of our gracious Queen and the honored guest of the occasion. Parad-
ing " *Prince Albert and the rest of the Royal Family,*" " *the
Army and Navy,*" and the " *Governor General,*" before you
reach the toast of the evening, is an unnecessary waste of
time, and mere superfluous *bosh*, designed for a particular end.
Now, sir, His Excellency Sir Edmund Head has lowered
himself to the standard of a political partisan, and to such a
degree that the friendly *Times* was constrained to remind him
of the old adage, which has almost fallen into desuetude, that
" honesty is the best policy." This is the opinion of every
citizen of Quebec and of every inhabitant of Canada whose
judgment is worth a straw in the matter. In the anomalous
position of the Governor General with reference to the part
he has lately played, it is obvious that his Health as a toast
is, at the present moment, most decidedly a *political* one, and
ought not to be offered at all, unless on some very great occasion, such as a banquet to celebrate some signal victory, or
the completion of some great national or provincial undertaking like the Grand Trunk Railway of Canada, when its omis-
sion, as respects loyalty to the Queen, might imply a negative

pregnant. It ought not assuredly to have been surreptitiously introduced at the recent entertainment to General Williams, as it necessarily merged into an expression of political opinion. Should any individual whose notions are more orthodox than *exaltés* on these matters, find himself accidentally present when an objectionable toast of this nature is offered, he will probably rise to it, and, however reluctantly, will go through the formality of drinking to it, so as not to interrupt the general harmony, and thereby defeat the main object in view. But no one ought to be forced into such a predicament. With respect to the demonstration in honor of General Williams, I feel assured that there was not a dissentient voice in the whole community as to the propriety of this public testimonial to a gallant and meritorious soldier ; but I feel equally assured that there were many who abstained from attending it under a well grounded apprehension that certain doings " above," would be aped in Quebec, and that they would be driven to the alternative either of seemingly toadying Sir Edmund Head, whose conduct they most unequivocally condemn, or of expressing their dissent in such a manner as to give pain to their honored guest, and thereby rudely to disturb the conviviality and unanimity which ought ever to prevail on such occasions. Mr. Mayor Langevin took an undue advantage of his position to preach up the Governor General in the interest of a party. In his seat in the House of Assembly he showed himself the obsequious tool of the members of a discomfited Administration, in moving a vote of want of confidence in the members of the Brown-Dorion Government before the ink was dry on their parchments, in order to favor the resurrection of the Macdonald-Cartier Cabinet and of their followers, who one and all, dared not encounter the ordeal of an appeal to their constituents. The glittering bauble of a portfolio, with the concomitant title of *honorable*, was the bait held out to induce him to sink the independence of his constituency, in upholding the eliminated " strategists."—It is said, however, that a certain M.P. from the lower part of this district, another auxiliary " shuffler," is about to walk away with the prize, as being eminently qualified, by his attainments and his administrative capacity and experience, to fulfil the duties of a minister of the Crown. His Worship the Mayor would do well to abstain for the future from playing such a false game and compromising the political character and the honor of the citizens of Quebec. They will probably not tolerate the repetition of such a piece of impertinence. If again attempted he may expect that some will cut the Gordian Knot, and make their appearance for the express purpose of counteracting such a shallow "chisel," and assert their right to approve or disapprove in an unmistakeable manner,—a most unpleasant recourse which they certainly do not covet, but which they may find themselves forced to adopt. The toast of the Governor General and of his beleaguered Cabinet are convertible terms and essentially partizan in their character and object, and will assuredly continue to be stigmatized as such, so long as Sir Edmund Head encumbers the soil of Canada.

THE

RECENT MASS MEETING IN QUEBEC,

AND THE TRUTHFUL MINISTERIAL ORGANS.

(To the Editor of the Quebec Gazette.)

QUEBEC, 13th December, 1858.

SIR,—" Accuracy " is a virtue for which public journalists in general do not conceive themselves particularly answerable. " All is grist that comes to their mill !" Their province is to cater for their readers, and impart to them the various *on dits* which may be in circulation respecting public matters. They certainly occasionally make broad assertions, but even then it must be presumed that they are made, or hazarded in good faith, that is, on the supposition that they *may be* true. Sometimes however, a statement of fact is put forth under such circumstances as to render it almost impossible to believe that the maker has not some twinging doubt as to its truth. Of this character is an assertion recently made in the " Morning Chronicle" of this city,—*that once respectable journal*, as itself designates the " Montreal Herald," viz. : " that the writer knew persons who were present at the recent mass meeting in Quebec, and that he was assured *that there were not present at that meeting, at any one time, more than one thousand persons !* Now, sir, the public in general pay little attention to the discrepancies between editors as to matters of fact, especially touching the numbers present at public meetings ; and in reality the importance of the occasion and the interest which it creates, depend more upon the cause and the object of the meeting, and the justice of its conclusions, than upon the numbers actually present. But really one cannot help being amazed at an assertion like the above, published in the heart of this city, where the occurrence took place but a week before. The cause of truth as well as of charity to the person duped, entirely apart from the importance or unimportance of the fact itself, require that a correction should be given, when that is possible. Here is the certificate of the keeper of the Jacques Cartier Hall, translated from the original now in your possession.

Quebec, 10th December, 1858.

" Having been requested by several persons to state the number present at the meeting in the Jacques Cartier Hall, on Wednesday the 1st December, instant, I certify that there were at least three thousand. I have been the keeper of the Hall since it was opened. I am convinced that I am not mistaken in the number, because during last summer there was an examination in the Hall of the scholars of the Frères Chrétiens school, on which occasion I issued 863 tickets of admission for three persons each ticket, all of which were delivered in on the day of the examination, making 2,589 persons. The Christian Brothers themselves gave tickets to several families, numbering at the least two hundred persons more, thus amounting altogether to *two thousand seven hundred and eighty-nine persons*, and the Hall was not so full as it was at the meeting of Wednesday, 1st December. It could contain ... dred more on the occasion of the examination of the F. Chrétiens School.

(Signed,)

OL. BIGAOUETTE.

The above establishes conclusively in the judgment of every reasonable man that there were *at the very lowest calculation three thousand persons present.* Moreover, there were many present who were so struck with the imposing appearance of the vast multitude that they went through the process of counting them in the best way in which that always difficult operation could be accomplished.—The hall, by its formation and division, afforded considerable facilities for ascertaining, approximately, the number present. We all concurred in opinion that there were at least three thousand there, viz :—

In the two side galleries, and in that fronting
    the stage............................ 800
In the corresponding spaces below the galleries
    where the people were much more thick-
    ly crowded.........................1000
In the entire body of the hall, where they were
    so densely pressed as to render it difficult
    to count them (some say 2000)........ 1500
In and around the stage.................... 150
                         ———
In all............................3450
                         ———

Now, sir, if the writer of the assertion in question knows one single individual who was present, and whose word is worth a straw, who will publicly aver that there were not more than *one thousand persons present*, let him " trot him out," or bear the imputation of having gratuitously and maliciously made a statement which will not bear daylight.

As to its having been an " utter failure," it is of course a matter of honest opinion ; but the man who makes such an assertion in this community, where the meeting in question is universally known to have been the greatest triumph of the kind during the last quarter of a century, must be exceedingly credulous, or he must be the " *vrai valet du diable.*"

The Toronto organ of the reigning shufflers has the effrontery to tell his readers that the meeting consisted of " manufacturers" and " hungry men out of employment and asking for work and alms, (*manufacturers and alms seekers*! !"`) When Charles the Second reproached his poet-laureate with the excellence of the verses made by him in praise of Cromwell, he replied, " Poets succeed best in fiction." The paid hireling of the Leader adopts the same principle in politics. When we see the public journalists of Quebec give extended publicity to the lying calumnies of the opposition organs of Toronto, which invariably asperse the character and undervalue the rights of the people of Quebec, upon whose industry these Quebec slanderers fatten, we are reminded of the caricature of General Jackson, who rides upon a Jackass, and Van Buren, who walks behind him, stepping in the footprints of the quadruped, and exclaiming, like the " Quebec Chronicle," " I tread in the footsteps of my illustrious predecessor !" The conduct and demeanour of the immense multitude present at the meeting of the 1st December was most orderly and respectable, and the harmony uninterrupted, save by the deafening shouts of applause with which the speakers were repeatedly greeted, and the loud and reiterated groans and hisses with which the names and acts of all and every the *dramatis personæ* of the late ministerial juggle were invariably hailed.

RUMORS OF A CHANGE OF GOVERNMENT

AND OF A DISSOLUTION.

To the Editor of the Quebec Gazette.

QUEBEC, 18th December, 1858.

Sir,—Dame rumor is now very busy with certain great
changes about to take place in the Government. Messrs. Cartier, Macdonald, Smith and Alleyn are about to be shelved
and their places filled up by a new batch of aspirants. Certain individuals among the Brown-Dorion party are indicated
as the forthcoming incumbents. Mr. Sicotte, Commissioner
of Public Works, is to construct the new ministerial edifice.
He is the Deucalion who is to cast about the bones of the
discarded " shufflers," in order to create a new race of con-
spirators who will secure to Governor Head his salary of
£7,777 for a few months longer. All which rumors were
floating about two months ago, with as much probability then
as now.—Another *on dit*, however, is going the rounds, which
though highly improbable, must not be suffered to pass without notice ;—that is, that Sir Edmund Head is to accommo-
date the new comers with a dissolution. Now, there is no
great harm in the spread of reports of change in the *personnel*
of the present Administration. They are believed to be ready
to betray each other on the first opportunity. They know that
they stand lower in public estimation than any Government
on record.—They are continually designated as a band of
shufflers and tricksters ; and it seems as if nothing could re-
deem the pack from the thousand and one opprobrious epithets
which are daily applied to them by friend and foe.—That any
one of the Brown-Dorion party should be such a nincom as
to entertain any such overture for a moment, is a calumny
which it may please the lacquey followers of the present tot-

tering Administration to disseminate, but which no man of
any knowledge of human nature, or sense of honor, would
credit for an instant, for two obvious reasons :—because it
would affix such a stigma upon the man who would thus betray his party while engaged in a life and death struggle for
the very existence of the constitution, as would eternally dis-
grace him in the estimation of every honest man ; and because his accession to the new Government would be the
mere acquisition of a lifeless trunk, denuded—*ipso facto*—of
every vestige of political influence, and the object of universal
contempt. There is not a single member of the late Brown-
Dorion Cabinet, who would not act as men of honor would
be expected to do in such an emergency, and who would not
indignantly spurn any such insulting offer ; and there is not
to be found one solitary individual in the large and influential
party who sustain them in the present crisis who does not
give them the fullest credit for such honorable intentions.

The rumor as to a dissolution being accorded to any such
new combination, acting antagonistically to the Brown-Dorion party, affords a practical illustration of their opinion of Sir
Edmund Head's statesmanship, and of the low estimate in
which he is held by his own friends and partizans.—*They*
ought to be the first to denounce such an idea and to shield
him from its damning consequences. However unconstitu-
tionally and rashly he has acted in sustaining the Macdonald-
Cartier cabinet ;—however much he may be implicated in the
conspiracy to call the Brown party to power with a view to
cheat or " chisel" them out of their places in Parliament ;—
whatever obloquy may attach to his name for having had recourse to the impudent mockery of entrusting the formation
of a Government to a member without any followers in or out
of the House, a refugee from the opposition ranks who chose
that seat in the body of the House which would best indicate
his ductility in respect of party combinations—a *sinon in
utrumque paratus*, determined to side with Trojan or Tyrian,
according to circumstances, without the dread alternative of
certain death which awaited the treachery of his less culpable
prototype ;—whatever amount of contempt may be entertain-

ed towards Sir Edmund Head for having essayed this shallow and disreputable ruse with a view to mask his " aboriginal" design to recall to his councils the *Macdonald-Cartier* faction, after having been metamorphosed into the more important and euphonic title of the *Cartier-Macdonald* administration ;—however low he may have sunk in the opinion of all virtuous men by his connivance at the desecration of an oath at which he performed the dignified part of quasi-suborner, preparatory to the enacting of the disgraceful shuffle by which the Commons House of Assembly were bearded in full session, their privileges trodden under foot and the people of Canada filched of their dearest rights ;—however dark and dense the cloud of iniquities which overshadow the closing days of the odious domination of the present Governor General in British America, we—his open and declared opponents, who have sworn eternal enmity to his reign,—do not believe that he could be guilty of such an outrage, not because we think there is no one among the miserable clique by which he is now surrounded who would venture to counsel a dissolution, could they escape scatheless from its consequences, but simply because we apprehend that Sir Edmund Head would not dare to perpetrate this culminating act of treason to his Sovereign, and treachery to the people of Canada.

One of two things ;—either the Governor General was a concerting party to the first resignation of the Macdonald-Cartier Ministry designed as a stratagem to produce the consequences which must naturally have been expected to flow from it, and which did in fact flow from it,—in which case the hardest terms in our language are inadequate sufficiently to characterize the turpitude of his act; or he was no party to the plot—which view of the case the divine principles of charity command us to assume as the true one.—Then, upon the latter assumption, the friends for whose benefit he afterwards made shipwreck of his reputation, must have wickedly placed him in that dilemma, in order—for their own selfish ends, to drive him to summon Mr. Brown to his rescue,—an opponent whom they had plotted to destroy afterwards by the aid of a few little tools whom they had at their command, and who were ready for any dirty work,—assisted by a few damaged followers who had escaped expulsion by legal quibbles, ministerial influence and strategy, and—" by the skin of their teeth !" and a few others who were the incarnation of every species of election fraud and of United States City Directors,—all foisted upon the floor of Parliament as a worthy phalanx to sustain a ministry of congenial birth and origin. The Governor General—having either as accomplice or victim —commanded Mr. Brown, in the name of his Royal Mistress, to assist him in administering her government in this Province, he was bound by that act, and by all the rules of honor and common justice, frankly and magnanimously to stand by him and his colleagues, and to afford them every constitutional remedy in his power to enable them to make good their position, and to shield himself from the many damaging imputations upon his fair dealing which were rife in Toronto during the crisis. By an adverse vote of the House moved by a willing instrument of the self-stultified cabinet, and carried by the votes of his fellow serfs, the Brown-Dorion Ministry were driven to resign and to demand a dissolution, which the Governor General peremptorily refused. It is now rumoured that it is to be accorded to their opponents ! !

It is but simple justice to the Governor General to say that we attach no credit to this report, and that we may be combating a phantom of the creation of which he is entirely guiltless. He cannot, however, and ought not to take umbrage at our pointing out, even hypothetically, the iniquity of such an act, and the grave consequences which must necessarily flow from it.—*Forewarned—Forearmed!* Twelve months have not elapsed since he afforded to the same party the *benefit* of a dissolution, which eventuated in the total overthrow of the Upper Canada branch of the Government, and the moral defeat and political extinction of the Twin-Premier for Lower Canada ; while five members of the then preceding Administration for Lower Canada, whom Sir Edmund Head and the Cartier-Sicotte clique had schemed to eliminate, were all re-elected by overwhelming majorities.

In the existing state of affairs we would ask—is there seriously a man *in* the Government or *out* of the Government who would dare to counsel the Governor General thus to "eat his own words," and to decree a dissolution for the same reasons, so to speak, upon which he had so recently refused it. It would be well before resorting to such an insane course to reflect upon its natural consequences. The Canadian people of both sections have already been the victims of misrule and the arbitrary domination of the minions of Downing street. Goaded to distraction by the repeated and not unfrequently insolent denegation of redress, they raised the standard of revolt and appealed to the arbitrament of the sword, in which they succumbed; but as a result of the insurrection, they obtained the absolute concession of constitutional government to be administered without the interference of Downing street or its cringing adherents in Canada,—a right which they indubitably previously possessed by virtue of the constitution, but which had always been unacknowledged in practice. The revolt or insurrection was put down; nevertheless calm, impartial history records that the *victory* was to the *vanquished*, and its fruits to the people of Canada, who will not now suffer the boon to be wrested from them, or its advantages to be impaired by any man, however high his position, nor by any "shuffler," however artfully he may skulk behind the scenes to conceal his individual responsibility. Let the Governor and each of his abettors beware how they or any of them abuse the authority and the privileges which the Sovereign on the one hand, and the constitution on the other have conferred upon them. Should they wilfully and corruptly violate the constitution and frustrate its honest and impartial working by means of a dissolution at the present crisis, the government of England and the people of Canada must hold them, each in his proper sphere, responsible for the act. Culprits of this stamp in other countries have been made to answer for their crimes by bringing their heads to the block, whenever the moral and constitutional guillotine of outraged public opinion failed to prove effectual. We tell them now, in order that they may be fully warned, that if any such nefa-

while the Earl of Elgin, for many years the constitutional Governor of Canada, is opening the vast empire of China to the commerce of the world,—the Queen's sceptre in British America must not be confided to men who pander to tricksters in order to secure a living and hoard a competency, at the expense of the justice and the honor of the Crown. The Queen's advisers have within their reach both noblemen and commoners of high standing, ability and independence of character, who are fitted to rule the destinies of a great country. By the treatment which Canada will now receive at the hands of the Metropolitan authorities will she stand as an honored British Dependency,—or writhe under a yoke. The other colonies, upon which free institutions and responsible Government have been engrafted, as well as those which look forward to those inestimable privileges, will be guided by the same beacon, and will either rejoice in the connexion, or sicken at the prospect of their future political humiliating condition. Let the colonial minister and his colleagues, whether they be Tory, Whig or Radical, look well to the key of the Queen's colonial empire in America. Let there be but one false step and away the whole fabric vanishes like a dissolving view, and nought remains but another historical illustration of the fate of Spain and Portugal. The reins of Government in the most advanced colony of the empire —the sheet anchor of English supremacy in North America, must not be entrusted to third-rate men. Their obscure baronets and Poor Law Commissioners must be disposed of amongst inferior commands. We will have no more pauper Governors in Canada. The times are too critical to risk the great interests of the nation by the promotion of mediocre or impracticable men through favoritism, or the stupid routine of a colonial roster. The advent of Sir Edmund Head to Canada was heralded by an unfavorable prestige derived from his nomination, as it was said, of a Chief Justice in New Brunswick against the opinion of his whole council. Had the colonial minister of the day been up to his duty, and had he known how to respect the rights of colonists in full possession of Responsible Government, he would have advised his Sovereign to present a "ticket of leave" to the new functionary, and to offer her refractory Lieutenant an appointment in a Crown Colony where dictation must be tolerated, and the "smallest favors are thankfully received." In the case of Canada Her Majesty's present Secretary for the Colonies, if he conscientiously desire the prosperity of the North American Provinces, and the stability of Queen Victoria's authority in her ultra-oceanic possessions, will carefully peruse the book of the history of the last six months in this Province, and coolly and impartially reflect thereon, and if after that he deem it for the interest and the honor of his Sovereign to prolong the incumbency of Sir Edmund Head in this portion of her dominions, we can only say that we shall be greatly and painfully disappointed in the character and tact of Sir Edward Lytton Bulwer.

RUMORS OF A MINISTERIAL POLICY

ON THE QUESTION OF THE SEAT OF GOVERNMENT.

(*To the Editor of the Quebec Gazette.*)

QUEBEC, 28th December, 1858.

Sir,—The political world of Canada is almost at a standstill. After a storm has come a calm. The resuscitated Government, upheld by the resurrectionist-in-chief and *his* constitution, still clings to the wreck in which it last foundered. The Premier, flattered by " Windsor Castle," struts his hour with all the arrogance of a *coq d'Inde*, and drives the ministerial coach with the recklessness of a ruined black-leg. Condemned by the people of Canada, and by the press of the United Kingdom, he consoles himself by telling over his rosary of *thirty* beads, presented to him by Queen Victoria, with the thirty letters of *Christophe Préfontaine, Verchères*, engraved upon them, in commemoration of the signal victory obtained by him over that opponent, and of the wonderful dodges by which he evaded any further engagement with him.—The blow aimed by the present administration at the constitution has recoiled upon their own heads. They have been reeling to and fro in search of a policy, and are now reputed to have found one on the question of the Seat of Government; and the very air is rife with rumors of dissensions in the wigwam on this point. They are to steal a plank from the reported platform of the Brown-Dorion party, and to establish the Seat of Government permanently in the midst of that blind and ungrateful constituency which ejected the premier at the last general election, and sent him away to beg, borrow, or steal *thirty* votes in the rural and humble constituency of Verchères, notwithstanding his brilliant promise to the " Free and Independent Electors of Montreal, the Commercial Metropolis of

Canada," that he would expend another sum of £100,000 of the monies of the Province in shifting, periodically, the mud and sand banks of Lake St. Peter, with a view—in despite (like his every other act) of the fiat of nature—to make Montreal the terminus of ocean, or "*salt water*," navigation. That was a great electioneering policy, and not so corrupt, by half, as many of the schemes and projects of the same man ; but the constituents whom it was designed to entrap, saw through the trick, and rejected the trickster. Now that the Victoria Bridge is about to add to the glory of Montreal by rendering it *impregnable*—" Windsor Castle" has no objections to retrieve his fallen fortunes by coming back to his first love ; but he will not accept the dictation of the Commissioner of Public Works, who, on his part, is too vain to follow the leadership of Mr. Cartier.

It behoves the members for the District of Quebec, and indeed all others who desire that the Seat of Government should be fixed in that place which is the best for the welfare, present and future, of the Province at large, and who have enough of honesty and manliness to express what they think —to pause and reflect upon the means by which the Government intend to accomplish their daring project. These are— first : by the votes of the ministerialists of Upper Canada ; secondly, by the votes of Upper Canada opposition members, to whom the choice of Montreal or Quebec (for that is the real question), is a matter of indifference, and who may be expected to be gained over ; thirdly, by the votes of the Ministerialists of the district of Montreal, as well as those of the Opposition members, who are expected to abandon every principle and to betray their party in order to deify Cartier ; and lastly, by the votes of the ministerial supporters *from the District of Quebec*,"—some of whom have already given proof of their subserviency, and who are all expected to sell their constituencies, in order to maintain that man in power, who has surreptitiously worked his way to the premiership of Canada in defiance of public opinion, and in utter contempt of every principle by which a right-minded statesman ought to be governed, and who, moreover, has betrayed a strong desire, had he the power, to rob Quebec of the eminent advantages which nature has bestowed upon it, as the chief seaport of Canada,—by sinking the monies of the inhabitants of this district in Lake St. Peter ; and who, moreover, has on every occasion exerted his influence to undervalue and degrade the district of Quebec and insult its people. The M.P.P.'s of this district who, if true to their mandates and their personal honor, ought to be unanimous on the question of the Seat of Government, and to stand out manfully for the maintenance of the rights of their constituents, are :—*Alleyn*, Quebec City; *Baby*, Rimouski ; Cauchon, Montmorency ; *Chapais*, Kamouraska ; *Cimon*, Charlevoix ; *Dionne*, Temiscouata ; Drummond, Lotbinière ; Dubord, Quebec City ; *Fortier*, Bellechasse ; *Fournier*, L'Islet; *Beaubien*, Montmagny : Hébert, Megantic ; *Langevin*, Dorchester ; *LeBouthillier*, Gaspé ; Lemieux, Levi ; *Meagher*, Bonaventure ; *Panet*, Quebec County ; *Price*, Chicoutimi and Saguenay ; Ross, Beauce ; Simard, Quebec City ; and Thibaudeau, Portneuf. The members italicised (*thirteen* out of *twenty-one*) are those who, while they are known heartily to detest their premier of the *thirty* unscrutinised votes, as well as his measures and his repulsive manners, are yet expected to submit in silence to his dictation and his caprice. *Expected*, I say, because, God forbid we should attribute to all these gentlemen any settled design to betray their trusts in order to gratify the ambition and the presumption of one man ; who—sustained for a time by unconstitutional means, obstinately persists in leading the Government of Canada, (notwithstanding its most emphatic condemnation of him, his policy, and his acts,) like unto a rusty, distorted, mutilated weather-cock perched on a church steeple, and perversely indicating the wind as blowing from one quarter, while the whole world is sensible that it blows from the opposite point of the compass.

Should it appear that Cartier & Co. are seriously bent upon the scheme in question, it would be well if all the constituencies of the District of Quebec would address a peremptory injunction to their representatives to oppose to the death a measure so hostile to their just expectations.—The project of fixing the Seat of Go ernment *at this particular moment* in Montreal, is a most audacious attempt to forestall the result of future events, in as much as the Union of the North American Provinces is rapidly advancing to its consummation under the auspices of the very men who are now said to be plotting to precipitate a decision in favor of Montreal, foreseeing that in such a conjuncture Quebec, by the common desire and for the general interest of all the Provinces, must inevitably be the Seat of Government. They expect that by a resort to the same barefaced corruption which accomplished the infamous Beauharnois Canal job they will carry Montreal for the Seat of Government of Canada, and that, like the Canal, it cannot afterwards be changed as the Seat of Government of the United Provinces, in contempt of the opinions and the wishes of the great majority of their inhabitants. Corruption stalks abroad in open day with all the unblushing effrontery of a harlot, and the question with respect to any public measure of general or local interest, affecting our political rights as a people, or our special rights as citizens, or with respect to the fitness or unfitness of any individual to fill the elective offices of member of Parliament, Mayor or Councillor, is not whether, on the one hand, the measure be desirable, beneficial, honest, wise, and patriotic, and the individuals in question the most eligible for these public trusts ; or whether on the other hand, the measure in question be a compound of rascality and selfishness, designed by a knave for some nefarious purpose, or the candidate a notorious impostor scheming for his own private interest and ambition ; but the sole question ever is—can such measure be successfully accomplished or the election of such a man secured—*per fas aut nefas ?*

Canada—one would imagine—must ever be the sport of tricksters. The advantages of Responsible Government were withheld for years from the Canadians, through the knavery and the falsehoods of officials and the family compact. One-seventh of the public lands were set apart to perpetuate sectarianism and intolerance, and the dominancy of one class of religionists over all the others by the same corrupt means, and subsequently three-fourths of their proceeds were squandered among Upper Canada Municipalities for the sake of popularity, thus recognizing a separate Crown domain for each Section in a United Province, and completing a double act of spoliation in respect of Lower Canada. The Canadian Trade act was another instance of the same system of imposture. The Union was consummated through fraud and treachery, and within late years a clause inserted with an intention to maintain equality in number of representatives between the two Provinces, was repealed upon the suggestion of some backstair knave, without the consent or even the knowledge of the people of Canada. Responsible Government, though fully acknowledged in 1841, was afterwards attempted to be wrested from the people by hollow-vacillating whigs and metropolitan emissaries and spies. Again, in 1858 the British Constitution, after having been unqualifiedly observed in practice since the Union, is set at naught and contemptuously trodden under foot, while the traitors are said to be sustained by the Crown, and some of them are entertained at Windsor Castle as persons whom the " Queen delighteth to honor." And now a question deeply involving the welfare of all the inhabitants of Canada, and pregnant with grave consequences to the security of all the British North American Provinces, and to British supremacy in this portion of the American continent, is to be disposed of by a resort to the same smuggling—dishonest system, notwithstanding the solemn pledge of the present Government, that no move should be made by them in this matter without obtaining first a fair and unbiassed opinion from the Legislative Assembly on the subject. How long is this system of successive rascalities to last ?

THE PENAL PROSECUTIONS

AGAINST MINISTERS.

MACDONNELL *VS.* VANKOUGHNET.

(*To the Editor of the Quebec Gazette.*)

QUEBEC, 26th January, 1859.

Sir,—On the 10th June, 1857, the Legislature of Canada passed a statute intituled, " *An Act further to secure the Independence of Parliament.*" Clause *two* disqualifies certain public functionaries and officers from voting at elections of members of the Legislative Council and Assembly. Clause *three* renders ineligible as such, all persons holding offices of emolument at the nomination of the Crown.—Provision *one* of this clause exempts from its operation members of the Executive Council, and certain public officers, of whom the President of Committees of the Executive Council is one—provided they be elected while holding such offices, and be not otherwise disqualified. Clause *six* declares that any person disqualified from voting in the Legislative Council or Assembly, presuming to sit or vote therein, shall forfeit £500 for each day he sits or votes. Clause *seven* provides that, " whenever any person holding the office of Receiver General, Inspector General, Secretary of the Province, Commissioner of Crown Lands, Attorney General, Solicitor General, Commissioner of Public Works, Speaker of the Legislative Council, *President of Committees of the Executive Council*, Minister of Agriculture, or Postmaster General, and being at the same time a member of the Legislative Assembly, or an elected member of the Legislative Council, shall resign his office, and within one month after his resignation accept any other of the said offices, he shall not thereby vacate his seat in the said Assembly or Council."

The Defendant, on the 29th July, 1858, then being a member of the Legislative Council, resigned his office of President of Committees of the Executive Council, which he held at the time of his election. On the 6th of August following, he accepted the office of Commissioner of Crown Lands, deeming himself exempt from re-election by virtue of the said 7th clause. He was prosecuted for the recovery of the forfeiture of £500, charged to have been incurred under the 6th clause, by reason of his sitting and voting in the Legislative Council after his acceptance of his second office. The legal proposition involved in this case is a very simple one. The Defendant was elected while holding one of the enumerated offices. On the 29th July—still holding the same office—he resigned it, and within one month accepted another of the said offices. Up to the period of his resignation of his first office, he continued *bona fide* (it must be so presumed,) to fill that office and to exercise the functions attached to it. When, on the 6th of August, he accepted another of the said offices, that act of acceptance is not impugned upon the ground of fraud or collusion, and it must therefore be presumed to have been made in good faith and with the full intention of discharging the duties belonging to the office. It seems to have been admitted on both sides that he has continued' to occupy that office, and there is no allegation or suggestion of any act on his part, subsequent to his acceptance, of a nature to shake the good faith of that act. The case of each Defendant on these penal prosecutions must stand or fall on its own merits. The guilt of one Defendant cannot be aggravated, nor—if defective—can it be rendered complete by reason of his supposed complicity with his colleagues, in perpetrating what is called the double " shuffle. " He was not prosecuted before a Criminal Court, as he and his colleagues and the Governor General might, and ought to have been, for a conspiracy to frustrate and pervert the operation of a statute, in which case the guilty acts of each might be invoked to prove the common design. He was simply prosecuted for an alleged infraction of a statute by sitting and voting in the Legislative Council after his acceptance of another office under the Crown. He is in every particular within the protection of the statute, and was rightly absolved from all liability.

MACDONNELL vs. MACDONALD.

The case of this Defendant stands upon very different grounds. He resigned his office of Attorney General on the 29th July. On the 6th of August he accepted the office of Postmaster General, (for which, no doubt, he was admirably qualified,) and on the same day, and within a few hours, he tired of that office, and returned to his old office of Attorney General. He was charged with an infraction of the statute, by reason of his having sat and voted in the Assembly after his acceptance of the Postmaster-Generalship, and also by reason of his having sat and voted therein, after his subsequent acceptance of the Attorney-Generalship. His liability on the first charge must be determined by the record as submitted to the Court for judgment. There is nothing in the mere act of acceptance of the first office, (weighing it at the moment of the acceptance) which impeaches the *bona fides* of that act, and the pleadings did not charge it to have been made fraudulently or collusively. But his resignation of that office, and his acceptance on the same day, and almost in the same breath, of the office of Attorney General, causes the mind to revert back to the moment of his acceptance of the office of Postmaster General, and has a most significant bearing upon the good or bad faith of that act. It was not charged, however, that the acceptance of the first office was *fraudulent*, nor that the pretended " *holding*" of that office for a few hours was also *fraudulent*; and the court, moreover, could not decide that matter of fact, however violent the presumption in its favor, without the intervention of a jury. It is for this reason, probably, that the court could not, or rather would not, draw any distinction between the case of Vankoughnet for a single infraction of the statute, and the double infraction case of Macdonald.

G

In the reasons assigned by Chief Justice Draper, which certainly savour more of judicial subtlety than true skill, considerable stress is laid upon the meaning of the word "whenever" as employed in the 7th section or clause of exemption from re-election in case of the re-acceptance of office within a month. Even Dictionaries are spoken of as throwing light upon the use of this word ; and since these novel expounders of legislative intention are appealed to, a few of the definitions given by some of them may not be irrelevant, Viz : Johnson qto v. "whenever"----*at whatsoever time,*----(not *as often as* :)---Knowles, Sheridan, and Walker, Ditto----" at whatever time,"----not----(*as often as* :)----Dr. Ogilvie, Imperial,----Ditto--- " at whatever time,"----(not *as often as*). So that passing over the fact of the resignation of an entire ministry, and that of their places being all filled up by others, the argument that the Legislature intended by the term "whenever" to confer a perpetual right upon any one of these public officers, or upon a whole cabinet to change places *ad libitum* and *ad infinitum*, if it have no more solid foundation than the import of this word as given in *Dictionaries*, is attenuated to an inappreciable degree, if it be not altogether absorbed in the immensity of the doubt, and the irrationality of the thing itself. Were this the case of a term used in a treaty, or in a contract or other written instrument, it would be interpreted according to its usual acceptation among the people using it, that is, according to *jus et norma loquendi*. In the present instance it is the Legislature which has made use of it, and that body may very properly be permitted to have a *jus et norma loquendi*. It is a matter within the knowledge of all that the Legislatures of all the countries with which we are familiar, generally make use of the clearest and most comprehensive terms to convey their meaning, and seldom or never leave a measure of time, quality, number or degree to rest upon a single word. A variety of words and expressions are almost invariably employed in order to exclude every possible cause of doubt or ambiguity, and this is what the vulgar style verbiage. The Legislature having its own *norma loquendi*, it is right to presume that had it intended the meaning applied by the

Judges to the term "whenever," it assuredly would have said "whenever," and *as often as*. Not having done so, the clause being exceptional in its provision, cannot be extended. A power or privilege must never transcend the plain and narrow import of the terms creating it, and more especially when it is to be exercised in virtue of an exceptional clause, it cannot be augmented, altered, strained or modified in any way. This is the Law of England and of France—of Upper and Lower Canada ; and if the Hottentots have a code or system of law written or traditionary, it will be found to have been adopted there by intuition, as being of the very essence of the science of jurisprudence.

When the Legislature empowered certain persons holding high offices of state to resign one office, and within one month to accept another without re-election, it must be held to have meant and intended,—first, when it speaks in the 7th section of a person " *holding*" any one of the enumerated offices which he is about to resign, that that *holding* should be *bona fide*, and for a sufficient length of time to render that supposition acceptable to common sense ; and secondly, that the acceptance of the new office should also be *bona fide*, and designed for the greater advantage of the public service. In the case of Vankoughnet who accepted but one office, no act of his, occurring previously or subsequently to such acceptance, is invoked to impugn the good faith either of his "holding" of the first office, or of his acceptance of the second. Not so in the case of Macdonald. The short time during which he occupied his new office of Postmaster General, and the celerity with which he flew from the Department of Letters to that of Law, affords conclusive proof of the character of the act of acceptance of his new dignity of Postmaster, and his sudden resignation of the same exalted position. His acceptance in the eyes of the Law, and of reason and common sense, cannot be otherwise considered than as a deception,—an evasion,—an act done *mala fide*, and not in the least with the intent which the act itself professed, of occupying that office. In one word—it was a sham acceptance concerted between himself and the Canadian representative of sovereignty, unmistakeably fraudulent and carrying with it no legal effect whatever. The same must be said of the " holding" by him of the same office ; that it was not *bona fide*, as contemplated by the statute, and therefore possessed no legal foundation or essence to enable him to avail himself of that " holding" as a *bona fide* stepping stone to another office.

It has passed into a proverb that " the Law abhors fraud," as nature is said to abhor a vacuum. No contract civil or religious, how solemn soever it may be in its character, or binding in its effects ; no act of the Sovereign herself, though consummated under her sign manual and attested with the great seal of the greatest kingdom of the earth ;—no deed however important in its nature and though engrossed and extended over many pages of parchment or paper, exhibiting a perfect specimen of caligraphy and adorned with all the seals and the arms of the most exalted contracting parties, and formally and solemnly witnessed by individuals of the highest standing ; in short, no act—deed—instrument—undertaking or stipulation whatever, though clothed with all the formalities of the law of the land, and contrived with all the skill and precaution of man, and executed with all the ingenuity of the devil,—can stand against the imputation and proof of fraud. In the hands of Justice, all, each and every of them, like the apple of the desert, collapse into dust, and disappear from the judicial eye as if they had never been, and are consigned to utter oblivion, save as to the odium which attaches to the perpetrators of acts reprobated by the laws of God and man. If this be the judgment of the law upon all fraudulent transactions in every civilized land, from the dawn of Roman jurisprudence to the present hour, by what other code of law or rule of morality are we to test the legality of an act done by a high public functionary deputed by the people to fulfil a public trust in which he is to sway their destinies for good or evil. The act of the defendant in accepting one public office for a few fleeting hours, and invoking the presence of the Almighty to attest the fidelity with which he swore to discharge its functions, palpably with the design of making it a mere momentary stepping-stone to the acceptance of another and a very different office, so as to evade the provisions of an anomalous statute, without precedent or counterpart, (according to their distorted interpretation of it) in the annals of legislation or of the administration of constitutional Government, was—to all intents and purposes—in the opinion of every man whose intelligence is above the level of the untutored denizen of the forest, a false and fraudulent act ; and if there could be found, from Dan to Beersheba, a Jury of twelve men who could, with a full knowledge of all the circumstances, find otherwise, the finger of scorn would be pointed at them until the closing hour of their existence, as men whose verdict had cast an indelible stain upon the morality and intelligence of the people of Canada, and made them and the boasted trial by jury itself, the objects of the ridicule and the contempt of the whole world.

As an indication of the fraudulent character of the acts of acceptance and resignation, it is only necessary to look at the marginal abstract found opposite to the clause in question, and which for laymen at least, and therefore for the people of Canada, as well as for any Jury having a knowledge of the fact, would have been conclusive evidence of the object of the Act. It would be in vain to tell twelve honest—conscientious men empannelled and sworn to render a verdict on the question of fraud, that the marginal abstract was no part of the statute, and that the words, " *Exchange of certain offices not to vacate the seats of the persons making such exchange*" written in plain English,—meant nothing ! ! Will any one be bold enough to assert that when the government framed that statute, and when it passed through the Legislature with these words conspicuously printed in the margin, and much more frequently read than the body of the act itself;—does any one imagine that the people of Canada will believe that the clause so labelled—and forming part of a statute entitled, *An Act further to secure the Independence of Parliament !*— designed anything more than a mere exchange of one office for another, simultaneously effected for the purpose of placing one particular member of the Government in a Department for which he happened to be more especially qualified, and this—for the greater advantage of the public service ! Or that the conversion of the late Premier, the Honorable J. A. Macdonald, one of the most eminent Jurisconsults of Upper Canada, and Her Majesty's principal law officer in that section, into a mere Postmaster and Superintendent of letter-carriers, was for the benefit of the public service ? I *assert* that when the statute was under the consideration of the Government it was repeatedly discussed by its members. That the clause rendering ineligible as members of the Legislative Council or Assembly any counsel retained by the Crown to prosecute or defend its rights, (which are those of the public,) in Courts of Law, was strongly opposed as injuriously restricting the choice of the Crown in the selection of the Advocates and Barristers best qualified for the task, and as inflicting a stigma upon the profession ; and that it was finally yielded as a sop to the democratic popularizing element in the Government.—There were also certain inelegancies of style adverted to (*disqualifying to &c.,*) which seem to have survived the strictures passed upon them. I *assert* that no other meaning than that found in the marginal abstract was ever broached or dreamt of in the mind of any one either in the Government or the Legislature, and that no more hideous monster could have been presented to the imagination of the very men who framed and canvassed the merits of that Law than the construction which they have since contended for and acted upon with so much effrontery and such gross ignorance of statute and constitutional Law. Just imagine a boat with twelve oarsmen, each in his appointed place, but possessing the privilege of making A. change places with B. when its proper equilibrium or the more regular stroke of the oars required it, and you have a fair illustration of the statute in question. But that after the boat, by their own mismanagement, had sprung a leak or been overset, and that they were seen piteously sprawling in the water, and that the unfortunate craft had been taken possession of by another crew,— the discomfited mariners should assert a right to retake possession after their bark had become derelict, is one of those propositions which drowning men alone could catch at, and which can only be offered to the proverbial credulity of the "marines."

The Globe has been fulminating against the Judges and threatening them with the "indignation" of the people of Upper Canada on account of their decisions. The onslaughts of the Canadian "Thunderer" are more remarkable for boldness than correct taste. It is not altogether orthodox to apply the epithets—ignorant, partial, knavish and corrupt, &c., to members of the judiciary upon whom their position imposes silence, and who alone in the community are debarred the right of self-defence. The upright—independent Judge will adhere to the stern law of duty *ruat coelum.* When conscious of having discharged it to the best of his ability, he will scout the very idea of public "indignation,"—even that of the redoubtable " Clear Grits," and will laugh to scorn any man or set of men who lay siege to him after that fashion. They are by no means, however, on that account to be shielded from rebuke when well merited. But if you apply strong terms of condemnation to their acts, you must not restrict yourself to mere abuse. You must show by sound reasoning, founded on facts, that your conclusions are just. Invective and argumentation must proceed together *passibus aequis,* and in that way it is perfectly allowable to bring him down to the level of the lowest delinquent who fails in his obligations to society, or commits a violation of its laws. Of this we have had repeated examples in that country where the judiciary is upheld and respected more than in any other, and whose people fully understand how much their fortunes, their liberties, and their lives depend upon the integrity and the independence of the Bench. The reputed editor-in-chief of the *Globe* who aspires to be the " coming man," and to be the chief adviser of Her Majesty in this Province, must temper his wrath with a little moderation and decorum, and not pour vollies of abuse upon high public functionaries without at the same time demonstrating conclusively that the lash is justly applied.

The opinions herein gratuitously enunciated are, of course given with the utmost possible deference. They are subject to correction and animadversion at the hands of any one who thinks differently. Moreover, the writer claims no exemption from supposed political bias. His leaning from the beginning —and which, in all probability, will subsist to the final *denouement*—was, and is, that the defendants ought to have been mulcted in the amount of the penalties as a salutary example to political malefactors in all time coming; and it is but right that the impartial reader should know that these views are obnoxious to the imputation of partiality towards one of the political parties now at issue. The avowal however, is made with perfect indifference as to the construction which the reader may be pleased to put upon it.

It is inferible, from the foregoing observations, that, as a matter of opinion, the parties prosecuting ought not to have withdrawn the case from the domain of fact; and ought not to have submitted it upon the mere legal skeleton contained in the pleadings. If this be accepted as the correct view, then the case is in a nutshell. It was eminently one for the province of a jury upon the question of the good or bad faith of the acts of acceptance, and of the " holding" of the intermediate offices. With respect to the judgment, however, it is sufficient that, in a penal action, a reasonable doubt should be thrown upon the case to cause the court to incline to the side of the defendants; and, in so far as regards the mere question of law involved in the pleadings submitted to the Court, the judgment—without reference to the reasons assigned in support of it—which are decidedly bad, may be correct; and an appeal may not afford any strong expectation of a reversal. But an appeal ought to be instituted and vigorously prosecuted upon other and more potent grounds than the mere hope of obtaining a condemnation against the defendants for a paltry amount of pelf. The prosecutions had a much higher and nobler aim, and the consideration of this part of the case trenches upon the conduct of the Judges, not at all in respect to what they *did* say, but what it is supposed they culpably omitted to say, in rendering their judgment.

When an unfortunate member of the community is dragged before a Criminal Court, charged with the commission of crime, and in the face of the clearest evidence, is acquitted, the rule of law and of right and justice is, that he should forthwith be permitted to go his way without stain or reproach. The law which presumes him innocent until he is tried and convicted, must *à fortiori* hold him to be so, when acquitted by a jury of his country. The verdict is his charter for the remainder of his life against any other charge based upon the same facts. But how often do we witness the spectacle of a prisoner about to be discharged from custody after having had a narrow escape from the fangs of the law, receiving at the hands of the Judge a severe admonition, unmistakeably predicated upon his supposed guilt, and the falsity of the verdict which has just been rendered by twelve men who are still within his hearing ; and how often does the man of rigid principles shudder when he reflects upon this violation of the naked, abstract rule of right, in lecturing an individual whom the law, his master, has pronounced to be innocent, and in telling twelve men sworn to find according to the evidence, that they have given a false verdict. Nevertheless, there are occasions when we feel that this rule is " more honored in the breach than in the observance," and when we are inclined to applaud the humanity of the Judge who warns the victim of depraved habits of the consequences of continuing his career of crime. Again—we continually witness, as well in purely civil as in penal actions, a failure of justice arising from a misapprehension of the law applicable to the pleadings or the facts of the case as submitted. What is the course usually observed by Courts of Justice on such occasions ? The Judges are the appointed expounders of the law for the benefit of all the Queen's subjects who are amenable to their jurisdiction. Their duty under such circumstances (and the independent, self-reliant Judge never omits it,) is to point out the error of the remedy which has been sought and the proper remedy which the parties ought to have pursued. In the exercise of this pretorian power, he explains the principles of the law applicable to the case as disclosed, and animadverts upon the grave consequences of the facts (had they been established), for the benefit of

H

the suitors, as well as the maintenance of the law and the purity of the administration of justice, more especially in cases affecting the public weal, and the rights and liberties of the people. Assuming that the judges were right in their conclusion of law, but that they were of opinion that the cases ought to have gone to a jury on the question of fraud involved as well in the acceptance of the intermediate offices, as in the pretended " holding " of the same, before their agile incumbents skipped from them to their old ministerial lairs, ought not the judges to have said so ? Was it not their paramount duty to have entered, even hypothetically, into the nature and character of the facts charged, and to have foreshadowed the probable or possible consequences, had a jury found against them on the allegation of fraud ? It is impossible to accept the hypothesis that the judges could be of any other opinion as to the real character of the acts done. "*Res ipsa loquitur*"—*ça saute aux yeux.* Upon pursuing the various reasons assigned by the judges in support of their judgment, it is evident that Mr. Chief Justice Draper went into a long introductory argument, replete with ingenuity, if not with sound law, and embracing matters and considerations, of which the relevancy is less apparent than the desire to expatiate upon them. The views of the leading—if not the master mind, are reflected with photographic similitude and complacent accordance in the comments of the other judges, betraying previous discussion among themselves on the different points involved. Chief Justice Robinson alone alludes to a jury, but quite significantly enough to show that that phase of the case had been considered by them, and that his mind had dwelt upon its importance. They knew that the eyes of all Canada were upon them, and that they were expected not to evade the main question, but to make a full and complete " deliverance" upon it in all its bearings. The parties prosecuted before them were the highest in the land,—ministers of the Crown entrusted with the administration of the Queen's Government in this Province, and whose every act ought to have been above suspicion. They were accused of betraying the trust confided to their hands for the welfare and the happiness of the people of this country, and of having, with the connivance of the Governor General, usurped certain high offices of state for their own selfish ends, in contempt of the constitution and of the veto of their constituents. Have the Judges thrown any light whatever upon the great constitutional question raised upon the interpretation of the statute in question, and which has so deeply agitated the whole people of Canada? They have not—they were silent. Their opinion now or hereafter, upon any such question, and in any such crisis, will be deemed for ever utterly valueless. Charged with the decision of so important a cause, involving the rights and privileges of the people of Canada, and the integrity of its constitution, they were bound to enlarge upon every phase which the case could lawfully or possibly assume under the authority of the statute in question, in order to prevent further litigation; and having done so, and while they absolved the defendants from responsibility on the law of the case as submitted, they were imperatively called upon to reprobate and denounce their conduct as utterly unworthy of men occupying their high position—a view which could have been forcibly illustrated by contrasting the doings of the Canadian ministry with the probable, nay certain course which the statesmen of England would have adopted under similar circumstances. Had they done so, they would have mantained intact the high character of the Upper Canada judiciary for integrity and independence, and would not have been obnoxious to the fierce onslaughts of the *Globe* and other prints. They would have given satisfaction to the people of Canada, who would have hailed the judgment—*dismissing their case*—as a triumph. A subscription limited to one *cent* each, would, with the rapidity of lightning, have poured in a sufficient sum to defray all the expenses of the prosecutions, and the people of Upper Canada would have rejoiced in such an opportunity of proving their zeal and their patriotism, and their contempt for the *pounds, shillings, and pence* part of the question. Had the judges adopted this manly, straightforward course, instead of idly quibbling upon the solution of immaterial provisions of the statute, there would have been no necessity for an appeal to England.

The moral verdict of condemnation against the shufflers and their master would have appeased the public indignation, and vindicated the laws and the honor of the people of Canada. After such a *victory* to the defendants so proclaimed, not the most presumptuous or the most reckless in Governor Head's ministry would ever again venture to mount the steps of their beleaguered old hospital. Its quondam inmates would have hidden their diminished heads in the most secluded spot to be found in the rural environs of Toronto. The whole fabric of government—the Governor General included—would have been paralysed—disintegrated. They would have fled the city as from a plague, their steps accelerated by certain tin-kettle appendages provided for them by an insulted public. Whithersoever they went, the scourge of an indignant public opinion would have perpetually hissed in their ears. Their abject, pitiable condition would have been their only safe-guard from indignity and insult. But the picture was too humiliating for such right honorable and honorable gentlemen on the one hand, and presented too great a triumph for the cause of truth and popular rights on the other. The judges shivered in the wind, and the defendants were absolved in silence ! ! !

It is therefore of the last importance that the case should be appealed, in order to prove that the Judges in England, while they may possibly confirm the judgment, will not imi-tate the Judges of Upper Canada in shirking the duty which they owed to the Sovereign who made them, and to the inha-bitants of Canada whose lives and fortunes are at their dis-posal. We have full confidence that the former will declare that had the presumption of fraud in respect of the acceptance and the " holding " of the intermediate offices, which, morally, is so strong, been legally established by the verdict of a jury, the defendants would assuredly have been mulcted in the penalties ; and that in any case their acts and doings will be characterised as disgraceful in men standing in the position of advisers of the Sovereign and representatives of the people, and moreover a most daring violation of the inalienable rights of British subjects.

WAIFS

OF

THREE YEARS.

WAIFS

OF

THREE YEARS.

PRINTED FOR PRIVATE CIRCULATION.

GLASGOW ·
Printed at the University Press,
By GEORGE RICHARDSON, 55 GLASSFORD STREET.
MDCCCLXXI.

PREFACE.

The longest of the following poems was written in competition for the Newdigate Prize of this year, gained by Mr. Mallock—I am glad indeed to be able to add, my friend.

I took up the subject at the last moment, spending little more than a forenoon and an evening upon it. Longer care would probably have made the piece shorter, would certainly have made the execution more perfect; still, the thoughts and feelings expressed were by no means the result of sudden conditions of mind, and I judge it best to print the whole without material alteration.

The other rhymes are, as the general title denotes, fragments saved by accidental expression in verse from years mainly spent in pursuits very different from such expression. I trust it is almost superfluous to add that none of them is intended to be taken as in the direct sense historical of my own life or of my own opinions. I would have them regarded as the results of poetic sympathy with certain states of feeling, sympathy I trust more or less enduring as those states are more or less worthy. Worthy of embodiment through art I of course hold them all or they would not have been the subjects of my verse.

J. R. A.

BALLIOL, 1871.

CONTENTS.

AT SUEZ.

Against mute wastes and melancholy sand
Twain oceans surge and whiten; all the land
Glows darkly in the hot South's pitiless glare
Day after parching day, sweet night-fall there
Falls never sweetly; fierce stars rise to burn
Above the desert, nor fond faces turn
Wan ecstasy from any dew-dim grove
To those old temple-lamps of crownéd Love.

Wide spaces sadden in the feverish dream
Of a long vanished wonder, of the stream
That poured in visionary triumph through
These ways, when once the hand of heaven drew
Exulting myriads towards the sacred fields,
Smote the far ranks and dimly rangéd shields
Of a wise people's strongest, while along
Low Red Sea marges eddying waves of song
Broke into exultation, telling Death
Had taken the slayer, and the people's breath
Came hard before the terror and the grace,
The shadow and the glory of God's face.

Yea, terribly the chosen passed that hour,
From all green places girding round the power
Of old Nile's calm forth-flowings, from the might
Of marble piled to heaven's starry height
And dominant widely o'er a subject earth,
From immemorial rites and mystic mirth
Dashed with red blood-stains, black with untold fear,
Where sworded lust in revel knew still near
The last, just, joyless Silence[1] ; and when war,
Power, pleasure, wisdom, all high things that are
In earth's low paths to long for, not again
Might give fierce solace to the despot's pain
By one Pain calmed forever, slowly borne
From streets far-thronging and fair gleams of morn,
Westward where Hell's pale bird and marsh apes bred,
Across the quiet Water of the Dead,
Mid gold and myrrh, within the caverned hill
He found a during slumber, dreamed round still
By all the story of Egyptian days
Burning in that sepulchral gloom to blaze,
Ten races' lifetime after, on hard eyes
That show the world still to herself seems wise
And still though grey is cruel.—Oh! not strange
That wild joy welcoming the wondrous change,

---

[1] The old story that introduces a corpse, as well as dancing girls, to an Egyptian feast is not without its meaning.

When through pale horror, drifted ocean spray,
And all thick night, was cloven out a way
To a great hope from forth the hopeless plain,
To a good sway—while every gorgeous fane
That groaned behind in desolation, drank
The blood of thousands ere her sand hills blank
Broke into pillared splendor—while alone
With pure Osiris, under earth, was known
The very name of Justice, still unspoke
Where prince, priest, god, made heavier the yoke
Of Misraim's mute life-labour. So they fled
Where flight was triumph ; on an army dead,
Wan faces and wet armour and white foam,
Pale morning mounting from her eastern home
Gleamed coldly, and against the glimmering shore
Great waves broke strange and restless—all the roar
Of yawning slaughter hushed—but mystery
Lit every ripple of that wondrous sea,
Curbed and cast loose divinely. Thrice dear then
The desert, after lonely haunts of men
Whom lust, not love, made brothers. Israel trod
Her bleak way to the terrible Mount of God
Breaking against the sultry, haze dimmed, blue
With bare scaurs buttressing torn spires wherethrough
The pallid lightning streamed ; above, the tone
Of trump—for war or holy service blown—
Now pealed from highest heaven, making plain
One King had power on earth. Wended again

Homewards a weary few, not Pharaoh's host,
Where never rain nor thunder wakes the lost
Land's fatal and luxurious quietness
With unhoped good, or burning plagues that bless.

   Oft, after, to these barren sands anew
The lingering might of ancient Egypt drew,
To face the northern foemen ; each low down,
In mellow eastern moonlight dimly brown,
Has gleamed with arms aud flowed with darkening gore,
When this broad highway of two worlds bore
A wasteful crop of death, through what long years
The Egyptian reigned and warred, until the fears
Of smitten wealth took hold upon his heart,
Till for high places, and the victor's part
Played long in gorgeous vanity, he found
A dim Fate cursing pleasure, mid the sound
Of falling empire, with the final doom
Of weakness dogging lust, till lust give room
Unto completed death.   Yet in his might
Once Misraim in these wastes watched heaven smite
For him, even him, the strength of Nineveh,
When murkily the mists of midnight lay
Swathing the Assyrian, and soft morning's birth
Found broken by the little things of earth
Bright lance and bow of the mighty.[2] Slowly so

---

[2] For the disarming of the Assyrians by a god-sent army of fieldmice,
see Herodotus.

Sennacherib's banded hordes, as billows flow
Rent by the rocks they burst on, home with fear
In panic weakness wandered, pressing near
To their empurpled warfare's period,   .
A feebler foe but how far stronger God !

The " River Dragon " yet a little while
Held sceptre in the towers of mystic Nile,
A little moment longer hung in air
The blow whose pitiless mercy knew to spare
For struggling subjugation, and long pain
That saw power near but grasped it not again.
Till, in what year the blood-stained madman ruled
On Media's imperial plains and schooled
Slaves with a madman's wisdom, Egypt felt
The first of wounds innumerable, dealt,
Through her frail breast-plate wrought with figured gold,
Beside Pelusium.   All her power grew old
And smiled and shook with palsy, when this path
Cambyses trod, to smite with mortal wrath
The giant, shapely, calm of old Gods set,
Gazing with eyes soft tear drops never wet
On gleaming temples and a groaning folk.
Here, on these coasts, the earliest thunder broke,
The people strove no further.   One more strong
Than Persia led his spears, with pæan song
And banners burning in exultant light
Of gold and crimson, since the orient bright

Paled dimly from before him, here to make
His own the land where daily words still wake
The name and memory of Ammon's Son.

Lo ! ever, as I gaze across the dun
Mists darkening over distant centuries,
All this bare tract between two sunny seas
That toss white splendor to the windy air,
Or lie in faint lit azure, calmly fair,
The whole is filled with surging tribes of men,
And thirsty blades and burning eyes again
That light with coming battle, where the sword
Is dulled in slaughter, and a stronger lord
Than Ares bids the passionate cheek grow pale,
The hot glance cold forever, and the wail
Of those at home, who share the spoil of woe,
Saddens the antique war-song's fervent flow,
Makes dim the embattled pomp of warring hosts
In wierd procession by Pelusian coasts.

When terraced Babylon ere long gave peace
To the last curse and brightest crown of Greece,
And Chaldee fanes mid blazing altars kept
The fiery Macedonian, as he slept,
Calm after war's wild revel, came no rest
Unto these sands, by heavy footsteps pressed
Of world-victors and free men made slaves.
Steadily rolled this way the steel edged waves

Of tower'd Rome's legionary tide that reared
Its billows ever, till no peak appeared
Of all the old world's pinnacles of power—
Rolled, and were shamed forever in that hour,
Here where the Thunderer's treeless temple crowned
Red cliffs and long slopes of unfruitful ground,
When noble blood was most ignobly spilt[3]
And one consummate sacrifice of guilt
Gave final consecration to the waste,
Where coward Death from primal ages placed
His dearest, earliest, latest-haunted shrine.
—Aye! not the dainty pilum soiled her fine
Point in vile slaughter of the Great turned weak!
The sceptred slave was wisely taught to wreak
A Roman vengeance on a Roman lord.
How should the curse have faded? Oh! what word
Can add to this last treason new dismay?
How need we linger more to watch what way
The fanged snake crawled across the desert sand,
Column on column, band on arméd band.
Keen Saracen, Crusader, scornful Frank,
All came, but how should shallow new things rank
With reverend, mystic, and most ancient deeds,
Wherein old faith against our new vaunt pleads?

---

[3] Pompey's head was the peace-offering of Egypt to Cæsar. As it happened, however, the deity was, if not "too good," at any rate too wise "to be propitiated."

Thus broods the dream of unforgotten things
Here, where the force of severed oceans flings
Its breakers on the desert.   Pageants leap
To glory after pageants, as, through deep
And limitless air, with golden glamour soared
The sacred bird, when bending priests had poured
The wine of pure libation, dark upon
White dust in yonder City of the Sun.[4]
But sullenly against the sands alway
The twain seas break their blue to surf of grey,
Unsatisfied and yearning as wide earth
Yearns for the deep calm and the holy mirth
Of some apocalypse, revealing peace
For travail.   Vainly?   Never then shall these
Move near to mingle?   From the red East burn
Clear wastes of water in the glow of morn,
And all the murmurs of the far gulfs bring
Such inarticulate sounds and joys as cling
To the gold-fretted hollow of a dome,
Where the rich East's wild splendor has its home
Below white flower-alcoves of marble, hung
Against the sultry air, and sweet lamps swung,
In that dim rondure of the vaulted vast
To shed a rose-like glory ; cries forth-cast
Where a barbaric people rises up
To greet their monarch as he grasps the cup,

---

[4] In Heliopolis was the temple where the Phœnix rose from its ashes.

Throned loftily on some great festival,
Or at the silver trump's melodious call
All sink again before him, bent as though
The spirit of a mighty wind did go
Unseen across the land.   Such wonders seem
To light on the large waves a gorgeous dream,
But, Oh! than any dream more fair, more sweet,
The musical white ripples at my feet,
Whispering of Eastern islets brightly strown
On gleaming seas, where odorous winds have blown,
Uncounted ages, and no haggard face
Has brought into that faery, marvellous place,
The insolent misery of man's new life,
Emulous peace and long, half-hearted, strife ;
But still the wild palm lifts her coronal
Where, through green valley-glooms, clear waters fall
To greet the summer ocean.   Ever come
Such marvels from the South.   Are ye then dumb,
Fair mid-land waves, that toss about the North
Of this slight barrier?   Ye! ye too, léap forth,
To sing the faithful words of antique rhyme,
To sigh the strong, sad tale of later time,
Whose burthen comes by Calpe.   Ye, wherethrough
Drove long the swarth Odysseus' weary crew,
Ye, that have gleamed about each storied shore
Where bright Powers moved and move again no more!
Myrtles still darken, up the seaward steep,
But all Eleusis' lights are laid to sleep,

Not any sound in air of God-driven cars !
Not any shout on earth of hero-wars !
Yet farther have your fruitless furrows pressed ;
—Wide ocean and the melancholy West
Send white-plumed armies to the sunrise sea,
From windy capes where shadows drift and flee,
Barring with purple, green sunsmitten surge,
Round my own island home ; or from the verge
Of that New World whereunto all men's eyes
Turn, waiting till some wonder shall arise
To illume a darkening globe—but mist alone
And wordy tumult o'er the wave are blown.

  Yea, many voices of one dædal earth
Swell hitherward with wailing and with mirth,
To mingle all in some great choral hymn
Whereat the hearer's vision should wax dim,
In the undreamed harmony of that strange song ;
But ever hath the barren curb been strong,
And, severing, marred the music.

                        Ages past,
A Pharaoh in the pride of empire cast
Forth from the bright sun as a little thing
Twelve myriad souls of men, that force might fling
The world's waves together. Murder failed
To work his master's will. When Misraim paled
Before the Persian, bitter eastern brine
Flooded the fruitful Nile. Not yet the sign

Of peace upon the earth and in the sea,
Rippled along the desert silently.

And now it ripples! Now great waters meet
To kiss each other! Orient glories greet
The stormy lands of sunset, now, when all
The wizard tales of antique splendor pall,
The light of starry gems and gold grows dim,
Nor any mage can gather unto him
The hidden riches of our monstrous earth!
Yea—all is gaudy tinsel, little worth,
That once was wonderful—a lie to hide
The squalid misery of blind crowds that bide
Death only, knowing evil and not good,
Since hot between them and clear heaven brood
The wings of lust that wears a diadem
With "Vanity" enwrought upon his mantle's hem.

So the East longed for, comes not, and the West,
What knows she now of joy and strenuous rest?
Shameless she flaunts upon her feverish stage
The pride of youth, the fainting powers of age,
And blankly echoes every word that slips
Across the closure of unrighteous lips,
As finding there salvation! Proudly came
Her castled keels together, with acclaim
Of far-reverberating self-applause
And gratulation, that she gave new laws

Unto the world's great waters, trusting so
To gather gold first, good might, after, flow
(Held She its deep springs in her hollow hand?)
Into dry water courses, till the land
Grew sweet with blossom.　Thus she vaunted then
Of Wealth and Peace and Pleasure unto men,
And how, far-off, clanged Fear's withdrawing wings.
The shout is hardly silent.　All heaven rings
Now with swift-fallen vengeance, with the cry
Of wrath, and pain, and poisonous agony
That breeds new sorrow.　Hope's face waxes wan,
For still she sees in all the life of man
Mere foolish moments of fulfilled desire,
Lost in one long repentance; yea, the fire
We dreamed divine, sinks where a dumb sod lies
Across the faces of the just and wise,
Set in a wasting sleep.　Oh! what remains
Now to us here, where Ruin dark-robed reigns
And fickle Change?　Alone is answer given
To pale hands stretching towards the hope of heaven?
And vain the faith with which we sought to raise
A truer hymn in unmelodious days,
With nations rangéd in the mystic choir,
While kindred voices of all men aspire
'Mid solemn aisles of silent centuries
Made musical in wise and perfect peace?
Does the masked world still mock us, and again
Toil men towards some dark end through manifest pain?

SAPPHO.[1]

Thou bringest everything, eve !
Thou bringest the mellow wine,
Thou bringest the goat from the rock,
To the mother thou bringest her boy,
But not to me my love !
Thou bringest the wandering bark
With curvéd wings of white
Into the little port,
The mariner leaps to land,
But thou bringest not my love !
Heëlios sinks far west
'Mid streams of pulsing light,
Which smite the pillared fane
Where the evening altar steams,
In depth of myrtle grove
Bright Aphrodite haunts ;
But up the rocky path,
Festooned with trailing vine,
No purple chlamys gleams
To my love-wearied eyes !

Selene follows fast
In the track of the greater glow,
But my panting bosom beats in vain
On the crimson-covered couch!
Alone, alone, alone!
O! how can joy grow cold?
Might I hold his heart to mine
I could plunge where bending skies
Bear oceanward the stars,
In the great World-clasper's clasp
By a mightier bond embraced.

1868.

MEETING ON THE WATERS.

I.

Lone in my shallop over the wave
Gurgling underneath each plank;
Far some of our squadron brightly brave,
Foam still floats white where others sank;
A fair boat sheweth on the sea
For an hour, but what is it to me?

II.

It came, it passed, and now again
Sweepeth hitherward amain,
Till my whole soul upward leaps
Eaglewise, to greet his eyes
Who watch there at the tiller keeps.
The two boats touch, and without a word
We join them with a scarlet cord,
A scarlet cord, of mystic dye,
As that on the Jericho harlot's house
Where Israel's plaguing hosts passed by.

Then two in one our voices rise
—One heart, one voice, and burning eyes—
Across the wave tumultuously ;
" Ne'er shall the bitter foam," we sing,
" Which blackening billows upward fling,
Gnaw through this link that knits in one,
Nor any more shall each alone
Before the wandering breezes run,
From North or rainy Southland blown !
Long have we each desired an end,
Whatever landing God might send,
As man desires a distant friend ;
But now we steer with pulsing veins
Over laughing water plains."

III.

So we sang, yet nevertheless
Again I float along
The unrestful wave in loneliness,
And the sacred fire whose flame was strong,
Yieldeth but a fitful ray
Of hope for the far-off landing day.

1868.

ANNIS AETATIS XVIII ET XX.

———

LAZILY landward a slow swell gleaming
Gently the floating sea-weed lifts;
Now wells the wave, now, backward streaming,
Pours through the dark rock's polished rifts.

Lie earth and ocean in golden slumbers,
Fulfilled with joy of deep mid-noon,
Divinely sphered in voiceless numbers,
The great world-harp's eternal tune.

O! forever to catch the beating,
Throbbing voice of the myriad strings!
My soul and dark-veiled Isis meeting
Flood with wide glory earthly things!

Rise I in strength to adore the brightening
Front that gleams through soft, grey cloud,
But to despair at its pallid whitening?
While in great weakness I cry aloud,

" Gods, fair Gods of the vanished ages !
God, whom the world worships still !
Names that man shouts in the war he wages,
Aiders unseen of the weakened will !

Ye of the dawn, why grow ye paler,
As the morning star through a shadowy shower ?
Thou whom they now name how help'st thou the wailer,
O ! dark through the dulness of a present hour ?

"Christ!" have they shouted, "great Christ our salvation !"
Wakened earth with the rapturous cry,
Now in hot darkness toils each nation—
Heap the thick clay, devour, and die !

    *   *   *   *   *   *   *

*Such the wailing and words of sadness
Leaped from my lips two years ago ;
I grub now as man thank the Giver of madness,
—Swine take the precipice in row !*

1868 and 1870.

SANCTA MARIA.

And canst thou say I did not love thee
Who gave a human soul for thine,
And idly perish to approve thee,
As eager eyes dream, all divine?

In Youth's hushed, happy ways I waited
A second birth, a nobler might,
A word of fire to send the fated
Feet stepping up the illumined height;

And, lo! a lucid brow's completeness,
Eyes starry, wondrous wreathèd hair,
Soft lips of all-perplexing sweetness
To close with kiss or move by prayer;

Luxurious chain of words low-spoken,
And murmuring laughter's pauses warm,
Strange fetters that might not be broken,
Left by light touch of hand and arm!

Self-alien in the eddying passion
I seemed, and all old things were new,
Transfigured from familiar fashion
In one bright mist of burning dew.

Still pure through pines the pale moon slanted,
I moved by ocean's ancient moan,
Watched noon's calm upland plains, nor panted
In the rapt worship I had known.

And bitter words for reverent wonder,
Darkened the depths of eyes once dear,
Heaven paled above, earth melted under,
Alone thou, Love, thou only, near!

Thou near, thou near! O! dark forever,
Planet of second birth to me!
Sweet influences—would I sever
The bands that fetter fatally?

1869.

TO THE UNKNOWN GOD. [2]

A land of sun-light ever falling clear
   Across the lake of life,
Where fairly ranked the shadowed shapes appear,
   Not stricken into strife.

I. FAUNUS.

Slowly amid the spacious world's splendor
   A child in wonder strays,
Whose large eyes flashing, back in beauty render
   The brightness of the days.
O'er plains that dimly in the distance fade,
   Through gloom of glimmering wood
He moves, and as the lyre young Hermes played
   Expressed its master's mood,
So his exulting voice and every gesture
   With cords of life's love bound,
Clad, as with riches of a varied vesture,
   The dim earth lying round;
And in that first warm flush of human feeling
   That knew—but not to sever—
The woe of Nature's vastness won its healing
   Fulfilled its dumb endeavour;

Till, mastered by the breaking wave that bore it,
    The marvellous life of man -
Sank down before the world to adore it,
    Rapt into wonder wan.
And strength, not strange but straight from nature drawn,
    Fashioned fair limbs and features
To the soft wildness of the musing Faun
    And blameless woodland creatures.

Dawn's glory fades; men toil beneath the heel
    Of darkened power endued
With lordship of the plain, through thickets reel
    A hot-eyed satyr brood.

II.. APOLLO.

Fallen the Son of morning from his place,
    And after him in turn,
Snatches the flaring pine-torch of the race
    A youth whose pulses burn
To drive their tide with all its mortal beatings
    Through the world's every vein,
Not covering of the face, but human greetings
    To sky and earth and main.
He plants his steps as among things not strange,
    His orbed eye flashes through them,
And, poised upon the wild chord's throbbing range,
    He sings himself into them.
Yet a far-hidden sadness chills the state
    Of splendid glance and tone,

Wrapped in the folded mantle of grey Fate,
  Upon a supreme throne;
Darkness above, and darkness writhes beneath,
  Howe'er with scornful gaze
A Pythian's pride may watch the gleaming death
  Sink in that knotted maze
Of the worm's foulness, yet the evil thing
  Dead, dieth not forever,
And, stained with loathéd gore, the Archer-king
  Serves by a northern river;
Till desperate youth, to scatter shadows thronging
  About the land of light,
Waves that wild flame with which the Orient strove
  To illumine lingering night.
Beneath calm stars he seeks with maddened longing
  The source from which he sprang,
While, under shadow of the mystic grove,
  Rapt Mænads' cymbals clang.
The turbid flow of feeling passes quickly,
  And leaves a cold life cast
Upon the dark earth's dankness, watching weakly
  The river eddy past.

III. JESUS ASSUMPTUS.

" Quid statis aspicientes in cœlum ?"

How shall we sing the heart that scorns all song
  And treads the weary earth

In loneliness of labour, making strong
 Its individual worth;'
That thrusts the Dumb God's outstretched hands away,
 'Quenches the morning star,
While things in blind glare of discerning day
 Seem only as they are?
Oh! let him, in his generation wise,
 Heap up the coinéd gold,
And let him to the fierce crowd's tearless eyes
 An alien world unfold,
And, labouring vainly in the fire a space,
 With thick clay load his limbs—
But mock not thou the misery in his face
 By any sound of hymns.

IV. SPIRITUS VERITATIS.

"Alium Paracletum dabit vobis."

Twin Toil and Science spread their wings at even,
 While, on the sacred hill,
Round whose huge bases, bastioned, water-riven,
 Pale waves are tossing still,
Full in the setting sun's mysterious glory,
 White robed and garlanded
With dew-drooped laurel, wreathed around the hoary
 Awe of his sovran head,
At last a victor over glooming fears
 Peals the triumphant psalm,

Touching again the lyre of other years
   In more impassioned calm.
Another's toil has traced the linkéd chain
   Of wisdom through the earth,
Traced it and failed, his is the final gain,
   The hidden heart of worth.
He holds all nature in his central soul,
   Sphered into rapturous rest,
Back from his brightening glance wreathed vapours roll,
   The shapeless shades that pressed
About the dawn's brief gladness, bringing tears;
   Yea, his exultant heart
Half-dreams it stands amid the strong young years
   That ages hold apart—
Dreams it is even now at the beginning
   Of days that die so soon,
And vainly loves what fragments it is winning
   Of that forgotten tune
The Faun sang in the forest, or Apollo
   Beside the Phrygian stream—
But, Oh! the morning's flushing does not follow,
   Nor hopeful Phosphor's gleam,
Hot, dusty hours of labour. Daylight fades
   About the evening star;
On Time's broad river brood the falling shades
   Where life floats, strewn afar.

1869.

IN THE HANDS OF GOD.

In the hands of God are we,
Idle words that plead in vain,
Idle tears that pour like rain,
Idle hands that stretch and strain,
In the hands of God are we!

Half we dream our workings free,
Laboured lines of thought succeed
Failure smites the crowning deed,
Then woe cries from utmost need
"In the hands of God are we!"

Tender hands as men may see!
Lo! the steps whereon we stand,
Lo! the long illumined land,
Pleasures we had never planned,
In the hands of God are we!

Better surely so to be,
Purpose from the brain is dead,
Wreaths we culled not crown the head,
Limbs are clad and white teeth fed,
In the hands of God are we!

1869.

TO THE PYTHIAN APOLLO.

O! God Apollo, the Python-slayer,
Rise for me!
Yet again make large thy might, and lay her
Where the blackness burns nor eyes can see
Swift hours flee.

Lo! Lord, how her foulness fills all places
With all plaint,
And white and flushed are men's poisoned faces
Where the bright earth crumbles beneath her taint,
Strong Gods faint.

Cursèd the gleam of her lurid glances,
Curst the breath
That sickens all life, and curst the advances
Of cold curved coils where the slime of death
Still clingeth.

Emptiest, idlest our curse! and the rather
Round despair,
For all her strong strained strivings gather
The damnèd grip and the darkness where
Sounds no prayer.

Stand as men tell thou used, Apollo !
Clad with light,
Here where lips lie, and fair shows are hollow,
And last and alone the adder's bite
Sets wrong right.

Hast thou slain indeed the Python, ages
Far agone?
Yet she lives, O! our Saviour, nor ought assuages
The pain perduring for suns that shone,
Deeds once done !´

Not anything save the one thing, great God,
Deadly, dear !
The one woe from which hearts redeemed would hate God,
—Still Saviour! leaving, though sorrow near,
Sleep too here !

For who shall sever sorrow from slumber,
Her one Mate?
Shall the cares that cark and the crimes that cumber
Waste ever? Lord of the painless fate,
All we wait !

1869.

DEAD ACHILLES.

"'Οτι μοι πλεῖστοι χαλκήρεα δοῦρα
Τρῶες ἐπέρριψαν περὶ Πηλείωνι θανόντι."
—Hom. Od. v. 309.

Lo! how darts hurtle through the flashing air
About the red, strife-trodden places, where
The battle burns beside Peleion dead ;
The battle howleth o'er that fair hushed head,
Gleameth above the darkened golden hair.

And must the wise Odysseus' wearied hand
Guard him whose glory seemeth yet to stand
Upon the rampart, rolled in terrible light,
Scatt'ring the victor foe to scathéd flight,
With voice uplifted through an echoing land ?

Ah, bitter woe, through his short wonning here,
Made keen the cold edge of that mighty spear,
Unsated all by darkly streaming blood,
Unslaked through wild Scamander's burthen'd flood,
Glaring about the slain friend's silent bier !

Good Hector fell, and Trojan women weep ;
Yea? How should youth's great love, turned sorrow, sleep,
Nor burn against the faces of the foe,
Slay many mighty for the one laid low—
The meaner mighty—and no reckoning keep ?

They weep the slain, cursing our slain who slew;
Yet his face's sad beauty shineth through
The sad, fair ages, as the morning-star
White in the dawn where thin cloud-glories are—
But fading not with freshness of the dew,

Wept by all gods and all men, in all time,
Clothed upon with all grace of antique rhyme,
All awe of ancient worship, all the love
That human hearts know, as they stretch above
Waste life to visions of a passed prime.

1870.

TO A LADY PLAYING.

WHERE pleasure laughs and lamps are burning,
While chill without, o'er pallid snow
A waste wind passes unreturning,
Sighing a restless song and low,
      Ah! sweet to hear
      The closes clear
Of Music's keen luxurious flow!

To watch white fingers swiftly wander
Across the silent-ranged strings,
Till each chord quivers into splendor
Of bright haze mantling mystic things,
      And all the lyre,
      An altar fire,
Bears up the voice of her that sings.

The faint eye fills, the cold cheek flushes,
As, poured in that melodious strain,
A flood of measured magic rushes
In on the soul like April rain
      —Ah! still to hear
      The cadence clear!
Let idle empires war and wane.

1870.

SONG.

Comes the sweet-voiced spring anew,
Fetching freshness, bathed in dew,
  Spring again!
Gold the green leaf glimmers through
Sunny mist and radiant rain,
  Spring again!

As bright days and wildwood tune
Burn and flow to fiery June,
  Ah! too Love
Moveth with the mounting moon,
Not—as she pines pale above,
  Not so Love!

Ever fervent, musical,
While suns flame and soft notes fall,
  Though in storm
These be set and silent all,
Lips and love with us are warm,
  Dear, are warm!

1870.

SONNET.

About the sick soul's fence rings night and day
A wordy babble of most vain opinion,
And human life, turned empress Rumour's minion,
In sullen slavery breathes half beast alway.

Men bandy wind-swoln thoughts, sing, preach, and pray,
Wax large and lusty, laugh, love, woo, and marry,
Make or break laws, and in due season carry
A brother's body to its mother clay—

Nor any of the grazing fools can say
Why he kicks at death and wantons long with living,
To the unimagined after season giving
Grace thrice sublimed from sun or clear star ray;

—Friends, if in heaven tongues still are hung to clatter,
Give me the grave, not crowns, palms, harps and chatter.

1870.

FRAGMENT.

Aye! restful, swathed under the cold, calm earth
In strange night-dew of death that giveth ease,
And other hearts gasp groaning for the heart
That groans not now forever, other eyes
Burn bitterly above the closed eyes chill,
Nor anything can move him any more.
Springs painted beauty buds to pass away
Where joys, tear-blighted, bud not from his dust,
And odour-burthened breezes, sighing sweep
Whither none knoweth—With the dead 'tis well,
Ill lingers with the living that are dead,
What although light's rich fancy fill all earth
And those sweet spaces of the evening heaven
With unimagined splendor? What though night
Pour music from each laurel wilderness
And moon-lit thicket, though by night and day,
Though the whole sunshine and all deep-dreaming night,
Soft rapture float on wings of a warm wind?
There breathes no bliss nor any glory gleams
On that lone soul whose sickness is to life,
Unpitied ever.

1870.

NIGHT AND LOVE.

Ah, Love, yon passionate star,
  Deep in dewy night,
Whitely flashes, flames afar
  To the painéd sight,
  Last her light
Swoons where undreamed splendors are,
Tangled gleams in viewless places
Spread against men's wistful faces,
Shadowy smiles and fresh tear-traces,
  Deep in dewy night!

Ah, Love, my own, most fair,
  Yet more nigh to me!
Heap warm shadow of thine hair,
  Sweet, until I see
  Only thee,
Only eyes love-kindled there!
Feel alone thy clinging arm,
Starry queen of mystic charm,
Fold me from all hard earth's harm—
  Close, more close to me!

1870.

AT NAIN, A FRAGMENT.[3]

A house in Nain, RACHEL *and a* CHILD.

Rachel (sings).   Noon burned on Shinar's parching plain,
   Through dust-clouds clouds of men as dust
    (Lord, in Thee we place our trust)
   Adored with dance and antique strain
   The golden idol of their lust,
    In Thee our trust !

   All wan by white fire-chambers he
   Whose greater godhead gave the god,
    (Yet our stay Thy staff and rod)
   Watched while they bare the holy Three
   In o'er the scorched and scarréd sod,
    Thy shepherd rod !

   But through the loud heat's blazing strife
   The voice of peace and glory came,
    (Saviour alway be Thy name)
   Unstayed, for still the Lord of Life
   Walked with them through the furnace-flame,
    Our Help, Thy name !

(RACHEL sends away the CHILD, who leaves saying.)

Child. Ah, but I may come again,
Soon again !
To hear how the good God saves from pain
Those that rest them in his love.
For you tell me of him ever,
Sitting while you spin,
And the warm sunlight streams in,
Through lucent leaves that sever
All the wide day's dust and heat
From the quiet at your feet.
Yes, you hymn in music low,
Not as fierce-eyed Miriam sang,
While the timbrels' triumph rang
And she watched the waters' foamy flow
Where those swirling surges ran
Above the great Egyptian—
But your voice is Sarah's, sitting
In the cool tent door,
Beside the son she bore
Late, and so loved,
Though scarcely witting
Half the care God showed in him ;
Yes, she gazed and gently chanted,
Under that shadow dim,
Of blessings heaven-granted ;
But Abraham held wondrous talk meanwhile,
And looked upon the faces

Of angel men sent down from unseen places
To cheer the faithful Father with God's smile.
And God gave me you to tell
All the things he doeth well,
Surely, so, I come again,
Soon again!   [*Exit.*]

Enter a WIDOW, *mother of Rachel's husband.*

Rachel.   My mother, his and mine, now rest thee here,
And shed the clear light, the most perfect peace
Of hallowed age upon us.   He cometh soon,
The mighty sun makes dim with too much splendor
The topmost crags of Carmel, as it passes
Behind those shattered barriers, warding earth,
To windless ocean's boundary of calm.
He cometh soon, even now his strong feet ring
Upon far winding ways that scarp the rock
Where terraced vines drink in long summer heat,
He comes, and quiet night descends on all,
Drawing her mystic temple walls of shade
More close about our fair shrined household life,
Whose glory sets not for its name is love,
And Love abateth never her dear toil.

Widow.   Yea! Miriam, never? and I tarry here,
Watch Love brood largely on your days and his,
His, who in times that turn to shadows now
Came as the crown and consummating gleam

Of inexpressible gladness to twain hearts,
Twain hearts, now twinned, while I abide to pace
The busy paths of unabiding toil,
The lonely walks of hunger seeking prey.
O ! Love holds empire, sitting crowned by you,
Love grasps the tool and labours still with you,
Love touches throbbing strings and chants to you,
But Love to me is uncrowned, palsied, dumb,
Through pale eyes looking on a land of dreams,
—A land of mists that shape themselves to men—
Or crazed by cavern echoes.   Every smile
Lightening across the calm of youthful faces
Half seems a mask the later time holds up
To mock some former reveller, till the gibe
Stings back against himself, both times being one,
And sad Hope seats her by the old Despairs.
Ah ! Rachel, Rachel, " clear light, perfect peace " !
—The light that blazes still before the man
Who from far merchandise has wandered home,
And finds not any home, but leaping flames,
And those who made it home finds nevermore—
The light that beats against his changéd eyes
Making the whole world black, the muffled peace
That bideth ever by the heart of him !

> *　　　*　　　*　　　*　　　*

(Rachel's husband has been carried in, killed in a quarrel with a
Roman soldier.)

Rachel.   Dead ? dead ? Ye flout me with mock-solemn faces,

You all laughed with us in fair marriage mirth,
When last those hills grew white against the winter
But now seen darkly under soft fall'n showers.
Dead! Let me through, it is not he lies there,
O! - -, husband, O! my love, one look!
Lift once your hand, but once, to waken me
From this dream's strangeness—Ah! the hand that ne'er
Spared one dear touch, though all the burning day
Strong toil had worn it, toil for me had tired—
Voice ever murmured in each tone that makes
The music and the magic of love's speech!

     *   *   *   *   *

(The bystanders have vainly tried to soothe her.)

Shall idle wrath burn only one the one,
This cruel spawn of a triply cruel breed,
Whose birthright is the bitterness of death,
To blast all beautiful and dear around,
Till full-fed Murder on his own foul heart
Draws that strange horror of the final blow
Whose doom immortalises guilt grown old?
    Just Might, that makest times and men thy tools,
Plague, plague the wolf-cubs wheresoever prowling;
O! slay them in the deserts of the South,
In the heaped ice and drift hail of the North,
Slay them in each green valley, and wooded pass,
And sky-hemmed plain of all the ancient East,
Let darkening Western waves gape death for them,

Sun haze and rain haze thick alike with slaughter!
Lo! they have trodden peoples underfoot,
Defiled thy temple, only Lord of Hosts!
Let West and East and South and North swarm in
To trample, pitiless, their pleasant homes;
Strike the swoln greatness of their gods aghast,
And show the faith, their fathers loved, a lie,
Then through all time let truth be false with them,
Until new nations mock the strong made weak,
The prudent witless and the wise men fools!

  *   *   *   *   *

 A Street in the same town; Lucius, *a Roman Noble, with*
  Attendants, *Roman and Greek.*

 Lucius. But again, why is the way so blissfully clear of
  wonted human dirt?

 Greek Attendant. My lord, the people through this restless
  land
Are strangely moved by words of many men
That style themselves the prophets of Jehovah,
And dole out him—the unimagined ruler,
So far as dull eyes of a stranger see it—
In bread miraculous to the poorer folk,
To the diseased, miraculous medicine,
Yea, show a third good more to gape against,
Though lying in the airy home of hope,
A coming king that long time shall not linger,
Perchance the promiser himself is he,

To give all value of the world's vastness
For this sweet herd to graze on.   Galilee
Even now of such a prodigy is proud,
Gets her food gratis in all desert wilds —
At least goes there to seek it, while such devils,
As plague peculiarly the chosen people
With large disease of sadness, from the triumph
O' the new Dionysus hurry hence to Hades.
That merchant whom we met some few hours back
Had heard of him, the Prophet, as not far,
And doubtless all the wisdom of the city
Crowds now to gain its crust and give its devil.

       *   *   *   *   *

1870.

THE PALMER.

"Lord, have not we left all and followed Thee?"

Ah! children of a shadowy Hope
And brethren of a deathsick love,
Your lives are large and your paths plain,
And music wheresoe'er ye move!

The joy of pleasant voices fills
Smooth lawns and slopes of garden ground,
Where warding wastes brood ever green
About sunshine and tuneful sound.

At eve along the antique wall
Soft notes entrance the dewy air,
For thorough gloom of guarded gates
The glow of living enters there,

To breathe a beauty through the courts,
And shed a shifting rainbow grace
Across the chamber's charméd gleam,
A splendor on the feast's high place.

Slow down the sweetly darkening stream,
While yet warm day fills half the sky,
The barge that moves seems moving not,
And tender tones delight and die.

Even when a world wakes to war
About the well-pitched tents of mirth,
He flings the jewelled armour on
And leaps athwart the battle's birth.

His war-cry rings, exulting wide,
He drives the foe before his spear,
Yea, though he fall he has lived well
And very death seems void of fear.

Ah! heaven the wisdom of the fool,
The worship of the godless one,
The praise that wells from forth the lips
Whose words owe homage unto none!

And I, my steps move strangely through
The desert and the homeless land,
I measure still the surgy sea,
Muse mid the untracked, unfruitful sand.

I press in many an alien town
Through babble of far-thronging streets,
Nor mother earth nor brother man
The burthen of my name repeats;

Not any smile to greet the glance
That burns below these drooping lids,
Nor grasp of any hand is given,
Nor any voice wished welcome bids;

And, Lord, in heaven thy palace shines,
My feet have sought Thee everywhere
On earth, but still the pale lips say,
The sad heart sobs, " He is not there."

1870.

SONG.

Let the laurel leaves
Through their own gloom glance,
Where white moonshine weaves
Mystic radiance,
    Let them glance, love !
Let the shaded stream
Murmur nightly moan,
Leave the clouds that dream,
Pure, and pale, and lone,
    To their trance, love !

Darling one, for we
Wist of holier light,
Know one shade to be
Of more deep delight,
    Wild delight, love !
Hear a richer strain,
Swoon in trance more still ;
Ah ! soft-panted pain,
Sobbed sweetnesses fill
    All warm night, love !

1870.

Over the mist-flecked mountain shadows,
Thorough the dim forest.
In the fair, grey-glimmering, dewy meadows
Your feet and mine have prest
Together, on autumn mornings gone,
When shivering star beam and gloom withdrawn
Wandered dark to the West,
Now streaming light, dear glories of dawn,
Dappled and swift as the glancing fawn,
Fill all with pained unrest,
Life of sunshine and sleep of peace
Over the desolate world cease,
My steps walk wildered, my soul is sad,
For the old tones sweet and clear and glad,
Not again, all years, shall warble through
Places of early dew.

1870.

THIS JULY.

Sweet fall familiar murmurs of the sea
Across the dewy close of day to me,
      This July,
Borne from ocean marges pale with foam,
Thorough the boscage and garden glooms of home,
Even as in hours long time gone by,
      This July.

Yea shall I turn me toward rest again,
Reach tired arms, lift a face that once was fain,
      One July?
Once fain, weak now and wasted as with fire,
Sick with days that sadden, pale with nights that tire,
Damp with the drops not showëred from on high,
      This July!

Long have I now wandered where the ways are dim,
Where a man meets not men at all to strengthen him,
      Though he die,
Though he live, no God anywhere on earth,
Living or dying nought at last he may deem worth
One pained heart beat, where hot pulses fly,
      This July.

Heaven mocks the tender child smile, turning bright
To the old spoiled splendor, to the lying light,
        Of a sky
Shrouding blackness, until even the infant face
Shudders for a moment, as one found in some wild place
Unaware—the deep curse knowing not as I,
        This July.

Old lips, that long have learned phrases of faith,
Bitterly seem drawn and writhe towards the dim face of death,
        Still most nigh,
Thus fair hope has faded from my heart at length,
Through the shadow weakness leads her crouching captive
    strength,
Through clear places time in scorn passes power by,
        This July.

And my soul now yearneth only unto peace,
Looketh but for lightening where all labours cease,
        All hopes die,
Day has been enough hard since the early dew,
When every opening flower was bright and wingéd breezes blew,
Now the air is heavy, petals shed and trampled lie,
        This July.

1870.

THE NEW DAWN.

Yes thou art mine my own !
Let the earth's strong places be
Tossed as the shifting sea,
With the blustering breezes blown,
Not wandering wave nor wind shall move this heart from me!

Tender the dear deep eyes
That gaze and melt to mine,
Dark hair, outwoven fine,
Against my shoulder lies,
A soft hand seeks more closely with my hand to entwine.

Lips longing strove to say
What both hearts wist of well ;
Though the whisper frustrate fell
We have chosen the better way,
A mouth that holds its peace things passing words can tell !

So are we ever thus,
The old life may loom again,
In her two hands toil and pain,
Not evil comes nigh us :
Bare branches are all in blossom, the rugged places plain !

1870.

IN A RUINED TEMPLE.

Swift, bitter, foamflakes of a fruitless sea
In sunless, whirling, eddy-gusts are blown,
About blank marbles standing drearily,
Or on the strong rock strown,
The rock unchanged alone
Over all the ocean marges gods and god-men have known.

Wild joy and reverence and entrancéd wonder,
That floated up the altar blazes, beat
Through rich choir systems or found veiling under
Blind rites that slaying were sweet,
Not ever again we greet,
Still is the world's helm i' the hands of ruining thunder.

O! cruel, cruel, cruel, the days that sweep,
Pale as torn mists, across the crags of time—
The gleaming, glimmering crags that all men climb—
Mists moving softly as sleep,
Or holy antique rhyme,
To slay with the utter death whose throne is on the deep.

They gather coldly against the eager eye
That flashes towards some one thing still deemed fair,
Some green place where the dews of morning lie,
The lights of morning air,
They cover it swiftly ere
Hot hearts teach ashen lips all the hopelesness of prayer.

1870.

A FANTASIA.

THOUGH hushed through the myrtle her nightingale's note
Dewy branches sway calm as in sleep,
Over faint lit shores mysteries moon-kindled float
Where surges sink back to the deep,
Colours glow, burn more brightly, where cloud wings hover
Above the blue gloom of a western steep,
While dim shadows wandering quietly cover
Wide places that pulsed and rejoiced with the sun,
—But of all dear things as I muse alone,
Life's Glory, and Wonder, and Rest they reap,
(Now turned is love's flow, mute her musical tone,
Like a dream the might of her day season over)
With the heart that remembers abides not one.

1870.

THE PICTURE.

It smiles not with the old charm I love
Nor breathes the tones I thrill to hear,
I miss the tender touch that drove
The world far off when one was near—
Yet is the still memorial dear.

I gaze and linger on the lines
That shadow forth all joy to me,
Till, dreaming o'er the unconscious signs,
I pass through them, seen nigh to thee,
The sweet place where I still would be !

Of all the Gods the oldest God,
Love, men adored when days were new,
Lives now times later ways are trod
But more unalterably true—
Passed unto heaven, yet all earth through.

In that most pure and holy place
Where broods deep glory of his wings,
I stand before thy pictured face
Turned from all waste unordered things—
Gold altars flame, a clear voice rings,

Floods with new all-unworded song
Courts of a consecrated heart ;
Not wide the world, time not long,
Not long, oh, Love ! from thee apart !
With dawn I kiss thee where thou art !

1870,

PHRYNE.

TO A BUST BY PRAXITELES.

I.

Ah! Phryne, Phryne, tenderly thine eyes
Gaze through long ages in mute marble whiteness,
And over all thy carven beauty lies
Some strange veil woven out of ancient brightness;
This heart, that pulses in a new age, sighs,
Seeks toward thy love-filled, love-enchanted glory,
Yearns where swift, pallid, splendor gusts arise
To sweep through gloom of half-forgotten story;
Wild tale! whose passionate meaning never dies,
But still the cold, antique, immortal flushes
With all the glow of pained love's fervent cries,
Through tears and smiles and wistful waxing blushes,
Unto some power abiding in the deep,
With life for name, and for last ending, Sleep.

II.

Men called thee Goddess, sinner now we call thee,
Press bitter lips, droop sad eyes at thy name;
What, if in years to come this should befall thee,
That some Redeemer put far away the shame?
That in the world made new some new light came,
And for all sinwoven, mystic, shifting, splendor,
Clothed thee upon with gladness free from blame,
As light of dewy morn triumphant, tender,
Filled with the swift sun's mastery of flame,
Filled with the dim night's music ever unspoken,
The gloom and glory that warring are the same?
—Yea?   And desire ye of these things a token?
Lo! now the strength and wisdom of the sun
Flood earth, ere man's day season of work be done.

1870.

NO DEATH.

There is no death, there is no death,
No death though life should be no more
Though vanity, the wise king saith,
Is all the world's treasure store,
Though weak all strength, and waste all breath,
Skies dull behind be dark before,
And sunlight o'er.

The gusty west, the sinking day,
Swift showers that stain a tossing sea,
Faint gleams of evening light that stray
Across the dim obscurity
And shadow of the eastern way—
What, where bare lands lie whirlwind-free,
Are theseto me?

Chill raindrift quenched the early glow,
Where peaked isles clove an azure deep,
Sweet streamed Ilissus ceased to flow,
Eleusis lights are laid to sleep.
No faint hymns now to rapture grow,
Or from the Foam-born's white fane sweep
The sunny steep.

Yea, have they faded, all these things ?
No music now in midnight stars ?
No worship where the laurel flings
To earth her splintered moon-shine bars,
Nor where the woodland water springs ?
No sound in air of God-driven cars,
No hero wars ?[4]

So be it, so it is, and yet
There mounteth up no bitter cry
To power in central darkness set,
To unseen wisdom throned on high ;
For long dead years no eye is wet,
Men wail the hours that wander nigh,
Not those gone by.

The hours that wander nigh they wail,
Then turn to stem the advancing time,
Greet with light love an antique tale,
Weave painfully with joy and crime
A newer web, Life may not fail—
Still marriage bells in music chime,
To mock sad rhyme.

1871.

IN THE FOREST.

WHERE bright summer sunlight glows
Through deep leaves,
Where wild forest odour blows
Through pine stems in dusky rows,
Scarcely grieves
The streams low voice, howe'er it flows ;
Dwindled in dim mossy coolness
From fresh Spring's exultant fulness ;
Where the faint-lit woodland weaves
Such a wreath for holy hair
As the young
Ages twined when life was fair,_
When among
Vines and roses everywhere
Men with maidens kissed and sung,
Dancing round each woodland altar,
Marble-bright,
Hymning strains that swelled to falter,
As daylight
Faded into fervent gloom—
Fresh blown night,
And the kind God smiling knew
Praise untold was still most true ;
—Yet should I wail the years that fleet
Were you but here in the shadow, Sweet !
I at your feet ?

1870.

IN THE CITY.

THE WOMEN'S HYMN FOR THE WARRIORS.

———

ALONG the ways of home war trumpets scream,
Then sink and sadden to a brave man's mourning,
As, winding ever farther, serried gleam
Keen arms in summer sunlight shifting, burning;
Our brothers' march to war,
The end is very far,
Ah! would we saw dear faces home returning.

Not now, not soon, not thus, O! never thus
Never, though hearts are true, hands do not falter,
Although through bittter battle-dust to us
The gods, besought, lead back a few, nor palter
With sacrifice and prayer;
The fate they follow there
Falls with a doom nor tears nor words can alter.

Yea, but they shall not fail, not this we fear!
Into their hands the hope they seek is given,
They work their people peace; though death stand near,
They snatch their time when ranks are crushed and riven,

To gain a wide land rest,
Nor shift a footstep lest   .
Not all return, not all the noble that have striven.

And thus they hold the joy, we bear the pain,
Not any breath makes quick our calm of sorrow,
Clouds loom above us as we wait the rain
And thunder of the inevitable morrow,
From bright Olympic thrones
Bend, O! ye crowned ones!
Sad hearts, from righteous heaven a little solace borrow!

1871.

DEAD ROSES AND SET SUNS.

FAINT odour of sweet roses dead—
Ah! those far days!
It kindles sunset splendors burning red
O'er alien ways,
As one bright sunset burned
Whose ashes are inurned
Over that home made holy by Love's sacred tread.

Faint odour of sweet roses dead
Wakens again
The echo of words softly, fondly said,
Heard now with pain
Across the bitter years,
Where the strange woodland rears
Dim masses to the fading of a bleak sun fled.

Faint odour of sweet roses dead—
Ah! Love, what more?
What secret memories blown whence old glooms spread
On Lethe's shore,
In surging overflow
Heap the wild gulfs of woe
About a heart left lonely and a prostrate head?

1871.

NOTES.

1. p. 19. SAPPHO.

The first four lines are translated from the well known fragment attributed to Sappho. Modern criticism holds them not to be by her, and further pitilessly mangles the words it has made orphan.

2. p. 29. TO THE UNKNOWN GOD.

This perhaps requires a word of explanation. It differs from the other poems in being not so much a work of free dramatic art, as a philosophy of History, done into rhyme. I begin not with marine jellies, nor even with our arboreal ancestor, but, where human history proper must always begin, with early eastern civilisation, and end with that whose completion can only be hoped for yet.

3. p. 44. AT NAIN.

My only excuse for printing this piece in its present fragmentary condition—or, rather this mere fragment of a piece, is that I do not just now appeal to the judgment of the public but seek the advice of friends. The drama, when completed, will deal with human life at the time when the diverse social systems of the ancient world were first crushed and melted together by Christian Persuasion and Roman Power.

4. p. 64. No DEATH. v. 3, l. 4, v. 4, lines 6 and 7.

It will be observed that these lines have been introduced into "At Suez" with but slight alterations. The circumstances of the composition of that poem, as mentioned in the preface, will explain this.

I have spoken of Art and of Dramatic poetry, in the preface and in these notes. It has been suggested that I should define the sense in which I employ these much used and much abused phrases. I regard the Artist as one who, because the whole truth is too wide for man's power to recognise as divinely fair, and because he would have something at least proved to be so that faith may be aided in answering for the rest, through sound, or marble, or colour, or words, sets before us beauty which is only a part of truth, and, therefore wholly a lie. A Poet is lyrical in so far as he does not know he is a liar; he is dramatic in so far as he is aware of this. The conscious liar is master of himself and of his works; by mingling many falsehoods he may very nearly reach the truth. The unconscious liar is slave to a few accidental sympathies.